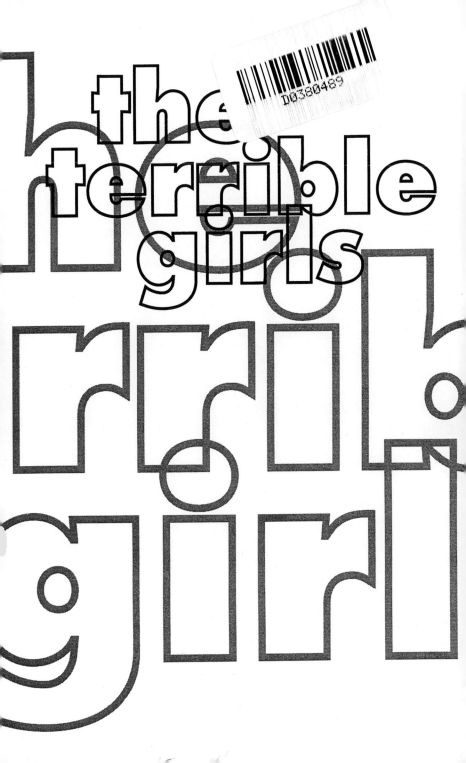

the terrible girls

Also by Rebecca Brown

Annie Oakley's Girl
The Dogs
Gifts of the Body

the terrible girls

a novel in stories

by rebecca brown

city lights books

© 1990 by Rebecca Brown
First published by City Lights Books in 1992

Originally published 1990 by Pan Books, London

Cover design by Rex Ray
Book design by Amy Scholder

Library of Congress Cataloging-in-Publication Data

Brown, Rebecca, 1956–
    The terrible girls / by Rebecca Brown.
        ISBN: 0-87286-266-6   p.   cm.
        I. Title.
    PS3552.R69/314/   1992   92-3391
    813'.54—dc20   CIP

Visit us on the web at: **www.citylights.com**

CITY LIGHTS BOOKS are edited by Lawrence Ferlinghetti and
Nancy J. Peters and published at the City Lights Bookstore,
261 Columbus Avenue, San Francisco, CA 94133.

ACKNOWLEDGEMENTS

"Isle of Skye" appeared originally in *The New Statesman*.
"Forgiveness" and "Junk Mail" were published first in
Passion Fruit (Pandora). "Dr. Frankenstein, I Presume"
appeared originally in *STORIA*.

The author would like to thank Hawthornden Castle International Writers' Retreat, The Browning Institute and Casa
Guidi for space in which to complete this book.

For seeing me through this American edition, thanks to
Mom, Tali, Patrick, George and Aldo.

This is for Louise

THE TERRIBLE GIRLS

THE DARK HOUSE

NEVER, YOU SAID, NOT me. Don't waste your time waiting.

But after a while you said, Well possibly.

Then after a longer while you said, Well maybe. But that whatever you might do, if you did anything, you'd certainly make no promises and one would be wrong to assume or expect. Then you cocked your head a little and said that if anything were perhaps to happen it would take a long, long time. But if one were around anyway and felt like it, one might wait.

This was your way of saying Someday. Of telling me to wait.

You said you couldn't even begin to think about it until after the conference. The conference was held every year. The job of hosting the conference rotated every year. You had been the hostess twice before. Once ages ago before me, then once when I first came to you, then now.

Yours was a good place to have it. Yours was a big and well-kept place of honey-colored stone. Mostly it was a long wide block like a country estate with wings on either end. There was a row of big sash windows with thick heavy curtains which you liked to keep drawn completely so, you said, the furniture wouldn't get faded. In the back was a courtyard with round, smooth white or grey stones, so perfect they seemed to have been washed in a machine, not just plucked from a river. There was a river past the courtyard, way past it, on the other side of the huge expansive yard of clipped green grass. The river, though you could hardly see it from your place, was wide and green-blue and rushing with water as thick as oil. Though whether the water felt oily you could only guess, if you cared to, having never been in the water. The river was not mentioned in your introductory tour of the grounds. All that was lush and rich and unmapped and untaxed, what you said you had no interest in, lay beyond the river.

From whence I had come.

Never, you said, not me.

You said you could never leave. You said you couldn't, you just couldn't.

Then wouldn't. Because you didn't have any interest. Because it was all right enough here and familiar. Then because we could scratch out a niche right here if we were discreet enough. Then because we ought to see how it went for a while anyway. Then because we seemed to be managing all right right here with all the nooks and crannies and hidden out-of-the-way places where we could rendezvous. (After a while one of those places was recognized as most convenient for our appointed rendezvous.) Then because of other reasons, reasons bigger than both of us. You said:

I don't have the papers.

You don't need any papers.

I haven't had the shots.

You don't need shots.

You ignored me.

More reasons:

You hadn't studied the maps (implying there were no maps.) You needed to work up until retirement, you'd invested so much.

Then, what if you went but when you got there you didn't like it?

Well, just come back.

Or what if you got sick or injured or tired out there, you continued, ignoring me.

But what would make you sick, I knew, was sticking around here forever.

Never, you said, don't waste your time waiting. Then you looked at me and asked, your lower lip pouting, coy, Don't you believe me?

I was the only one to whom you spoke about any of this. I brought it out of you. When you said, Never, I thought, You never have, but you will with me if I wait.

After I'd waited a long time, you sighed and said, Well, maybe. We'll have to see. Wait.

So I did. I was good at waiting. I could wait a long time.

This year was your turn to be hostess of the conference. I was glad. Always before I had missed you when you had gone, and when you had come back you were always so distant I had to wait for you to be with me again.

Every year it was the same people or at least the same kinds of people in the same positions. Though you said you didn't like any of them particularly there was a kind of comfort in the familiarity. Every year the host or hostess had to plan, organize, arrange, order the same things. You were good at it; you liked it. Actually what you liked was how everyone praised you and congratulated you and said how marvellous you were for organizing so well and how dedicated you were. (You thought they thought, but didn't say as it would not be polite, that your whole life was dedicated to your work, you had no personal life; you liked that appearance.) In fact though, as you told me with a dismissive sweep of your arm, you didn't like the conference. All the petty politics and run-of-the-mill repetitions made you sick and tired. And frankly you thought most of them were pretty stupid and boring, and certainly "intellectual cowards" (your phrase). You said you didn't participate because you liked to or got much out of it, but because you had to.

The first time you said this to me, ages ago, I said, Why do you have to, you don't have to. You looked at me like I'd just said, Where? when the tour guide was pointing to the Nile. Oops, I thought, but didn't say. I tried very hard to understand, to sympathize with you.

I also thought to myself that if you were going to get sick and tired, truly sick and tired, of what you said you didn't like, that I would stay and wait for that. Then I'd carry you away.

The same people, or people just like them only with different names, came every year. Whoever's turn it was to be host or hostess had a big job. I didn't deny that. I agreed it was important and time-consuming and took concentration. I never disparaged or belittled what you did. On the contrary, I offered to help. I'd do anything, I said. Could I help with the mailings or flyers? Accommodations? Leisure time activities? Meet anyone at the train station? Arrange things with the caterer? Sit at the welcome booth and say Welcome? Or at the information booth and say Two doors down on your right? Or meet you at night for our traditional appointed rendezvous and do what you asked?

But, you said, with your coy smile that was usually reserved for our traditional appointed rendezvous, and always reserved for me, my presence would distract you.

I said OK.

You lifted your chin slightly, trying to look noble and sad, and said that you had never had anyone before to do those things, you were used to doing them alone. Also you found it more efficient.

I said OK.

You said, Wait, when it's over everything will be different.

I said OK. I looked at you.

In a couple of seconds, you said, very sweetly, I'll be different.

I hoped so. I'd waited for it.

Then you cocked your head and said, Well, maybe I'll find something for you to do.

I didn't say, because I didn't need to, because you knew, that I'd do anything.

You knew that, though I didn't want to, I would have pretended for them, for you, that I was just another helpful civic-minded volunteer and not your one and only.

The conference went on a long time. Lectures, papers, seminars, discussion groups, morning coffees, evening sightseeing tours (optional), and lots of cocktail parties.

Given your organizational role, you weren't expected to come up with anything original, the way you would have if you were just a participant. You didn't have to be alone to think. Nor did you have to work so hard pre-planning. There were committees and volunteers and interns. You could have delegated, but you didn't. Some of the junk you did was busywork. You wanted everyone to say, My, she certainly works hard, doesn't she. Or, Look how much beyond the call, how marvellous she is.

I also think you wanted to overwork, to tire yourself.

When you and I met secretly, for our special rendezvous, you said to me, brushing your hand across your brow, your voice a shadow of its former self, that you were getting tired.

You don't have to do so much, I said.

You ignored me.

Are you not going to be well enough when it's time to go? I said.

Can't you see how tired I am, you pouted.

I saw you were tired of the stupid work. Everyone saw. But I'd given up trying to tell you to do less. I also saw you were sick, and more tired still, of pretending. Not only that you liked what you did, which you told me you didn't, but also about you and me.

I said, Look, if you think you're going to fall, at least let me be near enough to catch you and hold you up.

You didn't want anyone to see you, especially to see the way you were with me.

I should have said, Stop lying.

You found something for me to do at the conference. You made me the coffee-cart girl. My job was to deliver the coffee, tea, doughnuts and cakes. When there was no immediate coffee or tea need, I was clean-up girl. With these jobs I could always manage to be in the vicinity of you so I could know if you needed me, but far enough away so, as you insisted, no one would suspect. I also emptied trash cans, ashtrays, grease pots in the kitchen, glasses with residue of red or white or mineral water. I washed floors and did windows.

When you passed me in the hall where I was scrubbing on my hands and knees, making your floor the cleanest anyone had ever seen it, though you didn't appear to notice, I bowed my head and muttered, Ma'am. You muttered nothing to me.

I did all this because I understood, not only your "predicament" (your word) but also things about you no one else did, even you. When you said, Wait, you've got to understand, I said OK. I stuck by what I said.

You said that to me quietly so no one else could hear. Though no one else had ever been near when you spoke to me. You spoke to me when we were private and secret on our rendezvous, with hands and tongue and teeth and with – when it was open it was very dark – your mouth.

Yes, I said breathlessly, I could hardly say no when you had me like that, I'll wait.

I willed myself to wait. You were the one who didn't.

The convention had been going on for days. You had been so busy and had done so much work that you and I had not had time for our traditional appointed rendezvous activity. Though we had met. But when we'd met, we'd worked on organizing. Together we solved the little problems that arose each day about the conference. After a while, when the organizational kinks had been worked out so we could have started our traditional appointed rendezvous activity again, you said to table our meetings for a while because you were tired and needed some time alone. You didn't want to get too tired you said. I said, OK, I'd wait.

After the conference had gone on quite some time, you started getting bored. We hadn't met in a while, at least, not close-up. Though I had seen you every day, sailing from room to room, nodding your approval, clapping politely at others' findings or engaging in stimulating conversation, and generally holding forth until something even more important and/or interesting called you away. You always slipped away graciously. You didn't act tired at all.

I was with my coffee cart. My cart had two large pots – one with brewed coffee and one with hot water for those who prefer tea (we offered a selection of black and herbal varieties) or decaf. The cart had four boxes of one dozen mixed doughnuts each (glazed, twists, chocolate-covered, plain cake, cream-and jam- (blueberry, cherry, lemon) filled, and maple bars.) I was wearing my white apron over my black dress, dark tights, sensible shoes, and a small white cap, which actually looked more like a doily. I was pushing my cart down the empty hall to Seminar Room West lB. I was passing the elevator.

I didn't hear someone sneak up behind me, but I felt someone slap their hands over my mouth so I couldn't scream, and push me and my cart into the empty elevator. When the elevator door closed behind us the hands came off my mouth and turned me around so I could see who had abducted me: you. It had been so long since we had met for our rendezvous that I didn't recognize your hands. It was awful to have forgotten the touch of your hands.

We were in the elevator on the first floor, where my coffee was headed. You pushed the button to the fourth floor. The elevator door had a small window in it which people could see out of or into when the elevator was passing by a floor. But between each floor there was a space of about six feet where no one could see out or in. As the elevator went between the first and second floors, you yanked me towards you and kissed me on the mouth. Between the second and third floors you stuck your tongue down my throat and squeezed me hard through my uniform. I tried to touch you, but the window of the elevator was starting to show above the third floor.

Wait, you said.

You took a step away from me and dropped your hands to your sides. I looked at them. You looked at the buttons that lit up the floors the way strangers do on elevators.

When the door opened on the third floor, you stepped out without a glance at me. I looked at your retreating back while I tried to catch my breath and straighten the rumples you'd made in my uniform. As the doors closed in front of me, I saw, through the increasingly small slit between the panels of the door, and then through the window, you shake hands firmly with a couple of your colleagues. I waved to you but the elevator was going up so I didn't see if you waved to me.

But I told myself that you had waved, and that it was a secret sign for me: A little longer only. Wait.

It was so lovely what I saw, and so much what I wanted, that I closed my eyes between the floors and saw the sight of your hand waving in to me.

You were very concerned about doing things right.

But it was right, I said, what I wanted us to do. It was not new or wild or unique. On the contrary, it was common. We were going to be part of a fine and lovely and long and true tradition.

Not the greatest, granted, nor the best endowed, but a noble one in its own way nonetheless. Perhaps more accurately a heritage.

I knew this. But for you, in my time off, the time that any other time I would have met you for our rendezvous, I researched the history to show you that what I wanted us to do was right. Granted, the old pre-war encyclopedias didn't give much space to what I was looking for, and what they did say was inaccurate, but all modern scholarship supported it. Even the new edition of *The Children's Book of Knowledge Encyclopedia* had an article. There was a precedent.

I'm not like that, you said.

Yes you are, I said. I showed you an article.

I'm not like that, you repeated.

How 'bout this, I said, pointing at a picture. Right here —

I am not like that, you interrupted. How do you know that's not a lie?

I didn't say anything. I had photographs and documentary footage and tapes and records and videos and maps and I had come from there.

Besides, you said, even if you're not lying, that's not like me. I'm not like that. I'll never be like that. I'll never be like – you looked away from me, snapped your chin up and said with disdain – any of you coffee-cart girls.

I should have slapped you. I should have done you with a power drill, but I just sat there.

You had made me the coffee-cart girl.

Why did I keep waiting? Why did I keep believing that someday you would come around and stop lying? Was it only because I had waited so long already?

Partly. But also because I believed what you said. But maybe because I'd gotten so used to hearing what you said the way I wanted to that I couldn't tell what you really said. I wanted, when you had said to me, I'm not, I'll never, for you to have been lying. I wanted someday for you to stop lying and be with me.

One afternoon I was pushing my tea and coffee and cakes cart (cakes rather than doughnuts as it was afternoon) through the hall and I heard your voice coming from inside one of the rooms. I stopped the cart outside the room to listen. You were delivering a paper, nothing new or original, simply a recitation of some old stuff, the kind of thing any child or lazy undergrad could have copped from an encyclopedia. It wasn't your language. As I listened, I recognized phrases from *The Children's Book of Knowledge Encyclopedia,* the outdated version you'd grown up with. I could almost see, as you read out words that weren't your own, those old retouched black-and-white photo "reconstructions," edges blurred, of low-life hoodlums in rough, dirty clothes lurking around in creepy looking places. I think you really didn't realize that what you were reading from was not only obsolete and ridiculous, but wrong. I was embarrassed for you.

I set the wheel lock on my coffee cart and tiptoed over to look in the room. You were standing at the podium. I could see your profile from the back, lit up by the little podium light shining on your text. I looked out at the people watching you. They were shuffling in their seats and glancing at one another out of the corners of their eyes or over the rims of their glasses. Some of them sadly shook their heads. Some of their lips moved, whispering. They all saw through you.

There was one place where you departed from *The Children's Book of Knowledge Encyclopedia* article you'd copped. Everyone looked up from their laps when they heard you stutter. They were afraid you'd collapse – what if you were so tired you had a heart attack right then and there! I almost barged in to carry you away. But you caught your breath and continued your lecture. You said the words you'd stuttered over: coffee-cart girls.

I pressed my face to the glass and stared at you. You cleared your throat and adjusted your glasses and looked down your nose as if you were not quite used to talking about such things in company, other than clinically. You described the black skirt and white cap and sensible shoes I wore. You said the way one handled the coffee carts, the way one lifted the doughnuts from the tray, the movement of one's wrists and neck and shoulders when one poured coffee made it quite obvious what one was.

What should have been obvious to me was what you'd made me.

You were recounting, once again, the age-old questions: What makes one turn into a coffee-cart girl? Heredity or Environment? Dominant-submissive or submissive-dominant? Childhood clothing and games? How long one is breast fed? Or simply something very, very wicked? Then you launched into How to Deal with Them. Are they to be pitied or reviled? Are they to be treated as criminals, disturbed or handicapped? Everyone who was listening to you was polite. They shifted in their seats, stopped taking notes of what you said and started doodling to make it look like they were still taking notes, and also so they wouldn't have to meet your eyes if you looked out at them. You spoke as if your interest was purely academic. Though nothing you have ever done was pure.

I wondered if you actually thought the people you were speaking to believed you. Because the fact is, the people you were lying to, the colleagues you said you didn't respect in the first place, had figured you out ages ago. Despite what you thought of them, they weren't dumb. And they couldn't have cared less about what you were lying about. However, they were puzzled. Why is she lying, they whispered, Why is she saying such dumb archaic stuff? They tolerated you though, with the sweet sad sympathy of people who hoped they'd never be victim to the same self-delusion as you. They pretended they did not see through you. They felt embarrassment for you. They felt the pity felt for fools.

You'd always wondered what they'd say about you. What they were saying was, Poor dear, who does she think she's kidding, who's she lying for?

The person you were lying for was you.

At the end of the talk, there was polite applause, but no questions. They squirmed in their seats with embarrassment, hoping someone else would come up with some polite little comment or query for the discussion period. They all knew if they opened their mouths they'd only say, You don't really believe any of that stuff, do you? Or, Poor old dear, why can't you just admit it? They all were thinking, sadly, that they'd humor you as long as they had to put up with you. They knew, as I did not, that they didn't have much longer to wait.

That night there was a party in the big room. The room was supposed to be done up like a ballroom, but I couldn't keep my eyes off the things that had not been properly covered: the fold-up dining hall tables, the lunky cash registers at the ends of the self-serve cafeteria lines, the wrestling mats hanging on the south walls, the thick, heavy fire-resistant curtain on the stage. This was not a ballroom but a thinly disguised cafeteria and some-time gym. Beneath the smell of this evening's catered canapés, I could smell years of boiled cabbage and boiled potatoes and steamed hotdogs and sweatsocks. Everybody made a good show of not being aghast at the shoddy décor. But I couldn't help thinking of those awful high school dances, sock hops where everyone stood around nervous and sweaty and pimply under our Clearasil hoping we would, and praying we wouldn't, be asked to dance.

The lights were low. There was no furniture out except at the sides, long tables for the bar and canapés, and at the back, one long table for coffee and tea. I stood by the table at the back in my black dress and white apron and doily cap and sensible shoes. I served people coffee in china cups and saucers and asked them if they'd like milk or sugar. For tonight, we had real milk and sugar, not the little packets. I pointed to the bright shiny silver pitcher of milk and the shiny silver bowl of granulated sugar. I had my standard two pots going – coffee and hot water for tea or decaf. From time to time I'd partly lift the pots to see if I was running out and would need to refill one. Only once did I have to unplug the coffee pot and go back to the kitchen and ask them to fill it again. I didn't like to leave my table unattended, and I hated having to tell people that I was temporarily out of coffee but would have a fresh pot in a few minutes. I gave each person a napkin with their cup and saucer, a bigger napkin than they got, which they only got on request, with their drinks from the alcoholic bar.

Someone knocked the milk pitcher over. I thought it was someone who had had an alcoholic drink too many. I was pouring coffee so I didn't see who it was. The milk spilled on the table, wilting and wetting the crisp white pseudo-cloth table cloth. The milk spilt over the back of the table too. I wiped the biggest spill off the table, then squatted down under the table to wipe the wall and floor. When I was under the table, my dress pulled tight against me, I felt someone pawing my butt. I spun around as quick as I could, which wasn't very quick beneath the table, to slap the person who had taken such liberty with me: you.

I hadn't recognized your hands.

It was awful to have forgotten the touch of your hands.

My hand was raised to strike you, but you didn't notice.

Do you know what this party is for? you whispered.

It's – it's just a party, isn't it? I stammered, lowering my hand.

You put your finger to your lips. No, you whispered. You leaned close to me. I smelled your breath; it wasn't coffee. This is my retirement party.

I was too excited to ask you why you hadn't told me before. I blurted out, Then we can leave tonight.

You smiled, but put your finger to your lips to silence me. You pressed your hands on my legs above my knees. I had to steady myself with my hands on the floor, but it was hard scrunched beneath the table.

Tonight – I whispered, unable to contain myself.

Wait, you said, like a bad joke was over between us. Your eyes were bright.

When I opened my mouth again to ask you where we'd meet and when and the arrangements, you covered my mouth with yours so I'd be quiet. You knew a kiss would always, every time, keep me from asking, you from telling.

Wait, you said again. You squeezed my legs with your hands again then scooted out from under the table.

I sat under the table a couple seconds watching your feet, your calves and bottom of your skirt, walk briskly away. Then I shook off my daze of happiness and went back to work. I got back on my hands and knees and finished wiping up the milk. When I returned to pouring coffee, there was a sudden rush at the coffee table, like at an intermission. I worked hard and took care of everyone. I was so busy and so eager to be finished waiting that I barely noticed the people I served or heard what they were whispering about.

After the rush was over, the lights in the room began to dim. I heard the rattle of coffee cups against saucers. When I looked up everyone was adjusting their coffee on their laps, their bodies in their seats, more comfortably. There were rows of folding metal chairs with an aisle down the middle from front to back of the room. Someone had been very busy, perhaps as busy as I, when I'd been pouring coffee. In front of me I saw a roomful of backs of heads. When the house lights were dimmed halfway, one of your colleagues in a dowdy grey suit with thick, black-rimmed coke bottle glasses walked on to stage. She stood behind a podium and scratched the mic to see if it worked. The whole room crackled. She cleared her throat, leaning too close, then too far away from the mic. She said, Good evening, ahem, what a marvellous convention this has been. Then how well run and efficient, etc. and then how none of this would have been possible without the tireless efforts of one amongst us.

This time, for once, you hadn't seated yourself on stage or front and center so everyone could see you. This time, rather, you sat at the back of the room, pretending you didn't expect to be called up for acknowledgement. You sat in the last row in the room, the humblest and lowliest, the one in front of the coffee table, in front of me. I stood at work, my hands clasped tidily over my white apron, ready in a moment to pour a cup of coffee or tea for anyone who asked.

From where I stood, I could see your perfectly straight back. Your back is strong and square and white. I knew exactly what every bit of you looked like. When your dowdy colleague said, All the way at the back of the room... the people you'd always said you didn't give a damn about turned and looked at you and smiled. They couldn't see me standing behind you waiting in the dark. You bowed your head as if you were very humble and very touched and as if you hadn't ordered the chairs set out thus, as if you hadn't calculated exactly where you'd sit. Everyone looking back at you started to applaud. Your colleague on stage clapped loudly, her hands above the mic. She was actually quite sweet. After a generous round of clapping, she asked, Banner lights, please, and a banner above the stage was illuminated. I saw a roomful of backs of heads turn simultaneously. The banner said THANK YOU and GOOD LUCK and then your name, Miss – That's the part I looked at most. Your colleague started reciting into the scratchy microphone the official version of your long career of selfless, tireless dedication. She said what an inspiration and what an example you were. I stood at attention, my back to, but not touching, the edge of the coffee table. Part of me thought, If they only knew. But another part of me also felt a secret pleasure in knowing I knew the secrets of you that they did not. Despite myself, I felt a smile forming on my face, for you. But I hid it. Also for you.

Then your colleague asked the house lights to be cut entirely. For a second the room was completely dark. Though I couldn't see, I pretended I could, the back of your head, and that it turned around and looked at me. A spotlight was switched on above, to the right of your colleague. She cleared her throat as the light staggered over to her. She blinked into it, her coke-bottle glasses reflecting harshly. She fidgeted around in a flat grey purse she'd pulled from inside the podium. From the purse she removed a small package wrapped in festive, but sensible, shiny silver paper. About the size of a watch or a pair of pens.

I am most honored, she said slowly, trying to sound solemn, on behalf of all of us, to make this very small presentation as a very small token of our very great esteem and gratitude and respect for a most deserving one amongst us. Your colleague said, If we could possibly persuade our generous and tired and hard-working hostess of the past marvellous conference to let go her hard work for just a moment (knowing chuckles across the room), I should like to ask her to come forward. (Dramatic pause.) Miss—

I'd been so taken in by the theatrics of the darkness and the stage's single light, and of the long-windedness of the speaker, and of my eagerness to leave and of the practical business of leaving – is it too late to book a train? would I have time to pack a bag? how many pairs of shoes would you need? a regular or a traveller's size of toothpaste? – that I hadn't noticed anyone sneak up beside me.

But when your colleague called your name, Miss – you grabbed me.

You grab my hand and pull me. On stage, as she expects you to make your slow, hand-shaking way up to the front of the room, your colleague departs from the official version to add something new: you're about to embark on the dream of a lifetime. Because you've grabbed my hand, because you're dragging me out of the back, I don't hear the details.

Your free hand pushes the horizontal push bar on the door.

The two big metal doors close behind us. We hurry out into the night.

It isn't easy to run in my tights and black skirt and apron. I tear my white doily cap off and drop my apron as we run across the back courtyard. The white-grey stones look like a million tiny moons, smooth and round beneath us. You pull me across the courtyard to the clipped green grass. It's damp and my rubber soles squeak on it. I hear us breathing as we run, and behind us I hear puzzled shouts, Where is she, Where's she gone? Your moist hand, warmer as we run, is tight. It's tighter as you pull me to the river.

The land begins to slope down near the river. The ground gets slick with mud. You fling your arm around my back and we slip down the bank. Moonlight falls on the still river in a flat wide line. You push into the river, your body cutting the water into black triangular arrowheads. The black water climbs your calves and thighs. I stand at the edge of the water, wetness sucking around my ankles. The water is cold. I turn back to look at the big, light, well-kept place we've run away from. They've turned on the floodlights. The lights look harsh, accusing, against the honey-colored stones.

In the courtyard the conventioneers, your former colleagues, rush around looking for you. They open doors and windows. One of them picks up my apron and waves it, What's this? None of them notices I'm missing. A few of them have flashlights whose matchstick beams are weak against the sky. They look so small. Some of them run out to the grass. I wonder if someone will come to the edge of the river. They're so concerned for you. I feel sad for them. I almost want to shout to them that you're all right, don't worry. Why didn't you say something to them?

I want to ask you why but when I turn to you I see your back in front of me. Your hair and clothes are black. I almost can't see you against the black sky and the water. When you feel me looking at you, you turn around. Your face is white except the black slit opening of your mouth.

Come on.

I hesitate.

What are you waiting for?

I turn back to the old place again.

Don't wait.

When I look at you, you've turned around again. You are heading deeper in the river.

Black water is up to your back. I hear water lap you as it climbs your shoulders. The back of your neck is a white line; everything else is black. I expect you to dive in the water and swim but you don't. Your head goes under, your hands splash up. You're waving frantically. Your voice gargles: I can't swim.

I run a few paces then take a breath and dive into the water. The water feels thick and oily, my skin can't breathe. I open my eyes underwater but I can't see. My stomach tightens. I swim to where you went under but I can't see you. I swim below so long my lungs feel tight. Water starts coming in my mouth and nose. I need to swim up for air, but I feel something in my hands, your hair. I try to grab but it sways away like an underwater plant. I reach for your body though I can't see it. My hand finds your lips and eyelids. I cup my hand beneath your chin and pull you up towards the surface. When I go up my ears pop. I hadn't realized how deeply you'd sunk. When we break through the surface we're panting.

You've got to carry me across, you tell me, I can't swim.

I turn on my side and turn you so your back is in front of me. Your body moves very easily through the water. I reach my arm over your neck, across your chest and hold you by the pit of your arm. The skin inside my upper arm and forearm feels you breathe. The back of your head is in front of my face, your hair stuck up like spiky grass. I smooth your hair down, pressing my palm to touch you. You don't say anything.

Your back is against my hips, your shoulders are against my breast. I feel the slight, regular shift of you each stroke. I do not see your face.

But though we're close and though I'm pulling us, and though my skin is near you, there is some thing between us. The oily water coats us with a separating skin. What I touch isn't you, but what's between us.

The river is wide. We've stirred the water up. By the middle of the river, where the strongest current is, I'm tired. My head sinks. I sputter. You don't say anything. I don't know how long I can carry us.

When I feel the river bottom beneath my feet, I stumble.

We're across, I say. I hold you under my arm a moment longer than I need to before I say, We can walk the rest of the way. I start to take my hand from your neck.

I can't, you say. You hesitate. I can't walk. I sprained my ankle when I fell. You look away from me. You'll have to carry me.

I squat back into the water and hoist you on my back. You're much heavier than you were in the water. Your clothes drip on me.

I can't walk, you say again, as if I haven't believed you.

The bank rises up. It's a slippery climb into the woods. Tree branches scratch my face and arms. I trip over roots, in holes, but I don't drop you.

You don't say anything to me, but sometimes I hear you breathing as you sleep.

After a long time beneath your weight, I fall.

We've got to stop, I say, I'm tired, I've got to rest.

I start to put you down but you clutch my neck. You can't stop now, you say.

I'm tired, I need to rest.

Not here, you say.

We are in the woods. But there's no place near, I say.

There's a house ahead.

I can't see anything in the dark.

You'll see it soon, you say. You tighten your arms and legs around my body.

I'm so tired. You'll have to tell me where, I sigh. I readjust your thighs on my hips.

You point your finger in front of us, through the trees. This way, you say.

You lead us to the dark house.

No clearing is around it. All of a sudden, right up against the back of the trees, there's a picket fence surrounding an overgrown yard. The yard is around a huge house. The turrets and gables and roof of the house are sharp, and blacker than the sky.

I hold you steady on my back with one hand while my free hand lifts the latch of the gate. Rust cakes on my skin as the gate creaks open. I carry you into the yard. My feet find the remains of a path through the spiky grass. I carry you up the swaybacked wooden steps. The paint on the porch is chipped. The front porch swing is broken, one chain snapped so half the chair lies on the porch, the other dangles like someone hung.

When I knock on the door, your hand tightens around my neck. I lift the heavy iron knocker against the door and drop it. You whisper something I can't hear.

I knock again. After a few seconds, I try the doorknob. The door gives. It hasn't been latched. I push it open. I carry you over the threshold. I blink to adjust to the darkness. When I reach my hand to find a light, you whisper, No—

But I can't see—

Sshh! You put your hand over my mouth. Put me down.

I can't see where to put you. I can't see anything.

There's a couch over there. You point.

I walk a few feet on the creaky floor. You put your hand over my mouth as if you can stop the floor from squeaking. Your palm is sweaty. I bump into something. I squint down and can barely make out a settee. We're in an alcove off the entry room.

Down, you motion with your hands.

I take you off my back and set you down. I'm about to sit down next to you, but your fingers against my chest stop me.

I need to put my feet up, you whisper, Get a stool. You point in the dark where I can't see.

I follow your directions and trip over the stool. I bring it back to you and put your feet up on it. I start to sit beside you, but you shake your head no. I look at your face; skin grey, lips black, the tops and bottoms of your teeth between your slightly open lips, white.

You don't say anything so I try to sit again. I put my hand on the back of the settee behind your shoulder. I hear something.

I look up. When my eyes adjust, I see a banister, a second story hallway. From where I stand in the alcove, I can only see the bottom of the banister. The floor of the hallway is lit from the side, moonlight coming in through an upstairs window.

When I look at you, you're not looking up where the noise came from, you're looking at me.

There's a shuffling sound. I freeze. I'm afraid to whisper. I move my lips silently to you: There's someone in the house.

I hear the shuffling and look up again. I see a pair of slippers, the bottom of a dressing gown. I hold my breath not knowing if we should give ourselves away by asking mercy, we're only here for temporary shelter.

I look at you. You haven't looked up where the noise came from; you're still looking at me, apparently unafraid. I wonder if you haven't heard the noise.

There's someone in the house, I whisper.

You put your finger to your lips, Sshh.

The slippers upstairs shuffle again.

Get out of the house, you whisper to me.

I look at you, not believing you want me to abandon you.

I – I can't run, you whisper, pointing to your feet on the stool. You've got to go.

I'm so happy you want me to escape. You're thinking of me. This is a sign that shows me that you love me. Now that we're away from where we used to be, you can.

I won't leave you, I whisper earnestly. I close my eyes and reach for your hand.

I'll be all right, you mumble, pulling your hand away.

When I open my eyes, I see you less; the darkness of the room has gotten darker. When I look up, the figure upstairs is blocking the moonlight in the hall.

Get out.

I'm about to declare all my undying – when the person upstairs clears their throat. I gasp, then try to hide my fear. I look at you.

Your face betrays no fear.

The voice from upstairs says, Is that you?

Your face shows no surprise. Go, you whisper to me.

I look upstairs again. The slippers are facing us like this person is trying to see where we are. I start to pick you up and carry you away. Your arms are strong when they push me off.

Is that you?

You open your mouth in a way you never have for me.

That's when I realize it is not me that you're about to answer.

I grab your chin and turn your face to me. Whose house is this?

You lower your face.

I yank it up again. Whose house did you make me carry you to?

You close your eyes.

Tell me goddammit.

I don't hold you hard enough so you can't get away, but you don't pull away. You want me to ask you again. You want me to think I could get it out of you.

Tell me.

You open your mouth as if you're about to answer me. Instead you tell me, Kiss me.

I hesitate.

Quick, you say, Don't wait.

You know I will. Your holding out that kiss to me is making me make a choice which is no choice. I know there isn't time for both, an answer and a kiss. The mouth closed with the mouth won't tell. And you know I will kiss you, and in doing so, I'll let you get away with never telling.

I kiss you. A quick one on the lips; your mouth remains unopened.

Your hands push me away from you.

The steps creak upstairs. I look up between the banister legs and see the bottom of the housecoat, the slippers, moving. You turn me around by my hips and point my body towards the door I carried you through.

When I don't move, you stand up and push me. I gasp when I see you stand, your ankle cured miraculously.

Disarmed by your apparent cure, I can't resist. When you push me towards the door, I go.

Behind me I hear your voices.

Is that you?

Yes, I'm just coming.

You close the door behind me.

I stand outside the closed door of the house. Inside I hear a miracle – you walking.

I step off the porch. I look at the dewy grass and close my eyes.

I imagine I see the legs that you said couldn't walk, walk. I imagine I see you walking up the stairs, then down the upstairs hallway, through the door, into the room. I imagine you being inside the room. I open my eyes and look back at the house. It's dark.

But then, in the window of the upstairs room, the one I have imagined, a light flicks on, then slowly burns brighter: a candle. The light wavers, gold and slight, so I can see the shadows on the ceiling of the room. The shadows are of yourself and of the person of the house. They're moving. I watch the moving shadows of the two of you together. Suddenly they break apart. One of the shadows stays still while the other, yours, moves towards the window.

Your hand reaches up to the curtain. Your hand pulls the curtain partway closed, then hesitates as if it knows, because it knows, I'm watching. I wave to the hand but it does not wave back. But it leaves a small, thin opening where someone could wave through. I close my eyes and imagine your hand waving out to me. You leave that opening for me, a sign for me, a way of saying, Someday, if I wait.

ISLE OF SKYE

HELLO IS EASY. IT's the same most places. And if not, a smile or nod will do. But then again, in some countries, a smile means sadness; and greeting is expressed with an open mouth shaped like the letter "O."

I come to your house and drop my bag. Hello, I say.

Hello.

I wonder what the custom is, have I forgotten. You feed me tea and show me through your house. In both our countries, people sit on chairs. They walk on carpet or wood or cement or tile. They cover their walls with paper or paint. They put vases and mementoes on the mantels. Your house is different than I saw on my last visit.

In my country, you say, people live in homes.

That's like my country too.

So far so good.

You feed me tea. We talk about the miles and years between us. I pull out my Berlitz and smile, embarrassed when I have to look up your words. But you're patient with me and that's a good sign. I try to take my time and not to rush. Sometimes I look up a word you don't say, but just a word I'm thinking. I want to know how you'd think this feeling if you were thinking it yourself. Such as Desire, Longing, Want, Desire. I don't ask you.

The first time she left I knew she would not return. I was desolate. I did not want to remember her. I did not tell her. I forgot her. Which was possible because we'd never spoken. I had only my imagination to forget. She sent me postcards. She'd always travelled light. She returned suddenly and light. Carrying a Berlitz book and a passport. I was happy for the former. We sat down with it at once.

We try to talk and think we do, but we are each afraid. We know when we say blue that we mean blue. But maybe when you say blue, you mean sky. And maybe I mean water. Maybe we don't know to ask more than that. Maybe we don't know there's sky and chicory and Puget Sound. My eyes and navy uniforms. Maybe we don't know there's sapphire and moonstone and shower-wet slate, and that one shade from rain on oil. Maybe we don't know there's jay and powder, maybe we don't know skies. There are different colored skies in Texas, Windermere, above the Isle of Skye. We have to know more to ask more. My country's colors are these: tall green dark timber from Oregon; shiny black hard coal, Ohio; bright red crisp apples, Oregon; thick black fat oil from Texas; red dirt from Oklahoma; bright blue lakes from Seattle. New Mexico is dusty brown; Arizona, blister white. I don't know yours.

We share an interest in foreign tongues, the languages you need when you're away. But you have never been abroad; I've always left my home. Maybe our interests are compliments, exactly polar opposites. Or maybe they're just the same, two parts which once were intimate. We try hard to find out. We try to teach each other language.

I asked her where she'd been and she was going. I knew that she was going. I pulled out the atlas from the bookshelf in my study. We sat on the carpet. She crouched down, kneeled on one leg, pulled the other leg up. She leaned over the two-page map and looked. She spaced both her palms out flat in the air and made a circle above the book.

It's a big place, she said. She looked at me and smiled. Then she pointed, I go here and then I go here. I watched her hand trace down the page. The distance looked so easy. I've got friends here, then I'll go back here. Her finger moved to its left. Then in a couple of days I'll go back here. After that, here. I watched the shadow of her hand on the page, darkening the places. She tried to tell me about the smells of pine and salt and outdoor nights. Her fingers traced the routes that she had travelled. She said this map showed firm high mountains, deep cold lakes. But all I saw was a colored page. She told me thick black knots were cities. I asked her to pronounce the names of cities where I've never been. She told me New York, Philadelphia, New Orleans. She said Seattle, Cincinnati, Portland. She said Dallas and Chicago. They sounded exotic. Did she try to make them so? The names were written in letters of different sizes. The route numbers were as big as other cities. The next page of the atlas showed a country they said was a tenth the size of hers. The pictures were the same. This was my first lesson in the sorrow of our distance. I don't know if she knew.

We go for a walk so you can show me your country. We climb to the top of your favorite hill which you tell me has a view of your valley. They're long, low hills, yellow-brown and rubbed. They look tired and content. But it's foggy and we can't see anything beyond. You describe things that I must believe are there. I'd know more of a different thing if you'd shown me a map. You say, When it's clear that's the Gloucester valley. There you can see to Malvern. There's a big outcrop of Cotswold stone, and a cliff where people climb. We walk to the other side. Here you can see the Birdlip hill. Over there would be the Severn. There's a steeple there that's tall and white and slim. I can't see anything. You pull me to you facing straight. Behind you fog is rolling. Your hair and lips are dark against the pale greying sky. Your voice is slow, deliberate, printing deep inside me. There's a rundown mill and a tiny stream and sheep are grazing below us. There's soft wet brilliant hummock grass and sheep with thick brown wool. Smoke is curling from the chimney at the pub. There's yellow stone homes and dogs and cars. There's wet thick tufts of green. There's soil and sky and cities. Your firm cold hands are on my shoulders. Your hair and lips are dark against the fog. You just have to believe me, you insist, *This is landscape.*

When I feel your palms against my back, I do. There's something like faith and something like light inside me. If you told me we were anywhere, we would be. I hope my words for "landscape," "fog," and "sky" are the same words in your language. I believe you.

We're sitting in your kitchen trading stories. In particular, your life story and my life story, the things that happened since my last visit to you. You ask me about my first lover and then my first love. I'm dying to confess. In broken phrases I explain, and hope you'll see my floundering as the struggle of a foreigner with language. I hesitate with my Berlitz, trying to avoid your eyes.

The difficulty, I decide, is just in language, the time it takes to find things in Berlitz. I know, I *know,* that in your country, as in mine, our needs come from our bodies. In your country, as in mine, surely your countrymen all need the same, to eat and sleep and love.

In this pause I look at you. Here's what I'll remember: your dark hair framing your brightened face, every shallow wrinkle near your mouth and eyes. Your cheek. I want a map of these soft creases. They look like tiny deltas. Your eyes are hard and soft like warm ice lakes, the ones you've said are three hours north of your home. Then there is one moment when your lips part slightly.

When you raise your hand to me, I hesitate. In my country, this means I want you. Should I search through my tourbook, *The Ways and Customs of Your Country,* to find out what this means? But if I do I'll wreck the moment. Impulsively, I lunge. You pull me to you and when my mouth reaches yours, I think that I believe I understand you.

We give each other lessons, repeat phrases back and forth.

Blue is the sky above someplace.

Blue is the sky above someplace.

Desire is what you feel.

Desire is what you feel.

This kiss means this.

This kiss means this.

But no matter where we start, it's not back far enough. We can't explain "what you feel" or "this" or where is "someplace." We need to learn the first words first.

We try to get the basics. You explain mouth and thigh and knee to me. I define tongue and tooth and palm. You tell me what neck and breast and stomach mean. I say navel, leg and thigh. You give me the etymology of elbow and shoulder and back. I expound on fingers and flesh and thigh. You derive the roots of calf and rib. I trace back the sound of lip. You delineate the covert meaning of arm and ankle and wrist. I tell you mouth and breast and thigh. Every tongue is a foreign tongue. Your foreign tongue is mine.

This night we take each other to new countries neither of us has been to before. We are exhilarated, awed and lost. There are no maps.

I travel the cities from your knees to your thighs. My hands find avenues and lanes. This is a country road, a freeway, a round smooth cobbled street. Your skin has deltas, soft like silt. The earth moves, is shattered, comes together again. I find I'm not a foreigner when my tongue finds the warmth between your thighs.

She refuses to be photographed, convinced she's not a tourist. She talks about rates of exchange, conversion factors, post. One of the little expenses too many travellers don't take into account, she says wisely, is what the bank will charge for their conversion. It's a hidden cost, she warns me. I don't listen.

One of our hands is on one of our thighs. One of our tongues is on one of our breasts. One of our hands is on one of our backs. One of our feet runs up one of our calves. One of our tongues is on one of our necks. One of our mouths is on one of our ears. One of our hands is in one of our thighs. One of us breathes and one of us breathes.

Both of us learn this means Yes.

Your back is strong and square and white. Your hands are smooth and tough. Your tongue is like an underwater plant. My hands begin to glow with sweet thick oil. Your eyes change color. Your hands are smooth and tough.

We learn the meaning of the lack of sleep.

We make up words that we can't write or say, delicious, private, warm as thighs.

She's always travelled light and is proud of her travelling knowledge. She explains carefully how to pack her passport and her currency so pickpockets won't get at it. She keeps her passport by the bed, within reach of our lovemaking. Sometimes when she thinks I'm asleep, I hear her reach for it, run her fingertips on its old leather cover and sigh something I can't quite make out, I think another language.

We whisper syllables and touch. Our tongues touch and part, make words on fingertips, phrases from the tips of shoulders to chins, whole sentences and paragraphs on breasts. Pages on thighs. I think this time we forget what we know; that language is the only thing that lies.

This night we each wake from the same nightmare. Our stomachs are soaked in sweat. Neither can remember the dream. When I wake up I lunge for the lamp and put us in the light. She grabs for her passport. The room looks bright and bare as a bulb.

Are you all right?

Are you?

I lean into her my arms around her. We feel the sweat on one another's stomachs. She clutches her passport with one hand.

Hold me, I whisper. She tries.

I'm going to be ready, she says.

I'm afraid she is. I don't know where her pulse is racing.

Because in the dark when she's next to me, she whispers about transit. She says, It's like being in between. You could go anywhere.

I stroke her back and run my fingers down the soft bumps of her spine.

I say, But you aren't anywhere, are you? You're always in between.

She says, I like it right before you're there, when anything could happen. I don't ask if she's lost.

She speaks sentences from phrase books. In eleven languages she can ask when the next train leaves, is the water pure, where she can find a room. I know these phrases in only my own tongue, but many dialects, all rich.

You tell me, You are flexible, you're free. You wander many countries. You chat with all the natives. You move in and out of customs like a snake.

I protest, I say, You just don't know. This is the country I return to. I say, You are the country I return to. Insistent, I say, My home is not my home. You don't understand my freedom. All I have is papers. I tell you I am terrified of waking up in no man's land, my papers stolen, no one left to claim me or to understand my speech. My nightmare is that I'll be trapped without a phrasebook or a tourguide, without a map to your land or to mine.

You say, But that is freedom.

I say, But that is fear.

The only way I can look is forward or back.

I keep coming back to you. Everytime I leave, you say you know I won't return: I do. I come and come again to you. Each time I bring you more folk songs and tales from abroad. I think that's what you want from me. When will you believe I want to come back? When will you believe that I would stay?

You tell me "stay" means something different in your land. It's not a simple cut and dry translation.

Sadly, wisely, we avoid all talk of idioms. We do not mention syntax or semantics. We don't talk about variant readings, hidden meanings or the foggy subtleties of pun. We avoid the meanings of double entendres. Because we know, though we try desperately to deceive ourselves, that it *is* a matter of semantics. The language that we know means something real. We pretend we only know what we say. Language is the only thing that lies.

I'm afraid I think that what you want are my amusing stories from abroad. The next time I come back, I'll bring a slide projector, a carousel, some books, a pile of pamphlets, a stack of postcards for the fridge. I'll show you reams and reams of photos, some rare exotic artifacts, and talk about the habits of the natives. I'll bring you a goat from South America, a camel from the desert. I'll bring you a rickshaw and a pocket of pearls and a shell from Bora Bora. I want to present these things to you, to lay them on the mantelpiece. I want you to keep them. I'll become a curiosity, exaggerate my mannerisms. I'll be a parody to charm you. When will you believe these words and maps, these anecdotes are what I give, the way I'm trying to ask you, let me stay?

This is not what sustains her here. To keep her I must send her out. She is not happy still. There are ways she is that here would be a fool. We know the ways that we could not survive. Loving difference causes pain. We love what is different to possess it, to be whole. We want to be everything. The problem is, we can't. The problem is, the differences are different. Water and flame, brilliance and night, longing and fulfilment of desire. What keeps us moving is what keeps us sad, what keeps us moving is the want to be unforeign, whole.

Some words we try to translate just don't work. We can't agree. What you see as my freedom, I call fear. What I name strength in you, you label fear. I have to remind you of the beautiful cadences in your speech, the way your phrases fall like tides and rain and fog. You tell me mine's like lightning and like fog. Neither of us believes the other.

Will I get homesick or the travel itch? Will you get tired of being patient with my lack of fluency in your language? Your lessons with me cut into your life. You'll wonder is the payoff worth the effort.

You insist that I'd get bored; you're right. You tell me you'd get irritated; you're right. The fact is, we are different. Our union is a sharp specific point, the few words we've translated, the tiny border crossed.

I want to make true promises. I want to say when I'll be back. You hand me my passport, give me my worn Berlitz, and take me to the station.

In the train station, we stand apart, our bodies puzzled by distance. When I reach to hold you goodbye all our words rush up and out of me. I've forgotten how to speak. I touch your lips. I know this is a custom, is it yours or mine? Do you know what it means? Through the greasy yellow window on the train, I see you. You're leaning against a post and you are smiling. Your lips are mouthing words that I can't understand. I try to focus but I can't see. Are you trying to say you love me or goodbye? I start to raise my hand to you, then the train jolts. Did you see what I meant to do? Do you know this means I love you? Do you know this means I love you?

I take a train and then another train and then a bus and then a plane. I catch another bus, a cab, a train. I try to backtrack, circle back. I'm trying to throw something off my trail. Because I want a miracle. I want you to find me. I keep looking back, in rearview mirrors, over my shoulder, through fog.

At borders they check my passport, crumpled, stamped with my history. The nation of my origin is blurred, buried under colored marks of countries I've forgotten. And of yours.

At customs I declare these goods: three nights of love, a champagne cork, a picture in a garden. Two walks, a four day conversation, memories of hands. The scent of our flesh on my clothes, a memory of red. Some syllables that I can't spell, the tension in your thighs. The feel of hands, a sound of breath, the texture of your skin above your eyes. The magic feel of twice blessed flesh. The cold grey light of morning on your spine.

In this newly foreign country I've called home, my countrymen look different. I've forgotten how to say hello. I wake up at the wrong time, suffering jetlag.

I dream sadly and with longing of our transport. I long for you, I long for when we shall pass free through one another's homes. But this is a dream from which I awake.

I wake as if I were with you. I leave this narrow bed and walk streets I remember only dimly. I try to read the roadsigns and recall my native language, my own tongue.

In your land, it is morning. You're making tea and going out to work. I wander the darkened foggy streets alone, pretending in the dark half light I'll see you. The sky here now is foggy orange, the false light of the streetlamps.

I'm lost in a city whose name you can't pronounce; I think it is my own. Your country's maps spell this name differently. Will you recognize the post mark? Will you recognize my hand? Who'll translate the maps for us? Do you know this means I love you? Do you know this means I love you?

JUNK MAIL

I GET ALL THIS junk in the mail. It bothers me. The audacity of anyone to think they have the right to cram their shit into my mailbox. I throw it away.

On the other hand, it is about the only thing I ever get. Other than bills, the odd postcard from people I know on fascinating vacations, late Christmas cards, letters from my aunt in Wichita Falls. Letters I would forward to you if I knew where you were: "No Longer at This Address." Not much, in other words, worth writing home about.

So I toss it into the pile that continues to grow, daily, by my desk. Someday I'm going to throw it all out together or make a bonfire, something severe and beautiful. Meanwhile it gets to be a mess.

I hate the thought of it. Obviously everyone in my apartment building is subject to the same invasion. People all over town, all over the country, the world. Just think of the waste – the paper, the person-hours, the effort the postal people go through toting it around. Think of their blisters and sunburn, their aching shoulders. Think of the money stores pay those damned fools to design and package and disseminate this shit that no one wants to buy, that no one even wants to know about.

I think of warehouses upon warehouses, acres of the same Pay'N'Save booklets with detachable coupons, the billions of Safeway flyers advertising pot-roast specials through Friday, the special trial offers from *New Times,* the Christmas in July sales at Fred's Easy Mart, the slick magazine formats from god-knows-where with three color printing of bronzed baby shoes and plates with the Presidents' faces. I think of how much more room there'd be in the world without it. I think of fields and open air, a different and more easy kind of room.

It's not just the excess that makes it bad, but excess without reason. The bottom line, what it all boils down to is: *I don't want this shit.*

Have they ever asked? Do they think I'll believe their impossible promises, their idle threats: You May Already Be a Winner, Order By Midnight Tonight?

But I wonder.

I begin to glance at them. Gradually at first. Never more than one per batch, and only the interesting looking ones. I start opening some of the glossy ones with the really with-it graphics, the fat ones that feel like they contain a free sample inside. I open these clandestinely, tossing the rest of them into the ever widening pile by my desk. I feel almost furtive, until I remind myself that my interest in this is purely academic, research so I will know exactly what to say when I finally get around to writing the huffy, indignant and scathingly articulate letters to the Boards of Directors of these companies that plague me, when I finally tell them, with great finesse and sharp and righteous wrath, that my mailbox is not just anybody's into which they and their sleazy bulk-mailing morons can ram anything they feel like, yours sincerely, etc., etc.

I imagine the guy on the other end of my very pointed and very personal epistle: a fat cat, the Chairman of the Board, a big beefy guy in a pin-striped suit, his college tie loosened, his sleeves rolled up, him chewing a soggy cigar and juggling fourteen conference calls from New York, L.A. and London all at once. He's standing at the window in his 50th floor executive suite in Chicago looking out over the dim grey cityscape, his back to me. I see the back of his head, his bullish neck. Will he read his important private mail? Will he read my desperate message? I think he must. I see him sigh, his heavy shoulders rise and fall. I think he will. I see him turn, his thin and graceful neck. I think he already has. I see his cheeks, so high and fine. I think he has. I see his collar is loose, like yours. He has. I think he's you. I see his nice brown eyes. He is.

So.

I know why I'm getting all this junk. It's you – sending me a secret message, the only way you think you can get to me through all that is surrounding you, what you've built up.

Darling, why don't you just give me a call?

I look through all of it. I search for your secret message in the fine print underneath the unbelievable offers, the 150 valuable coupons, Sizzling Summer Savings, and Dollar Day brochures. There's nothing I can recognize of you right off. On the other hand, what if I really am a winner already? What if I order by midnight tonight? You want me to know this, don't you?

But I won't get distracted. It could be a trick. It could be you wanting to see if I'll turn my head as easily as you always did – I never did – if I'll let my attention from you lag. Though I have never, ever forgotten what we're up to, our true purpose here.

I know there's a message in the junk mail you send to me, a secret clue of what you want from me, a hint of how to find you. The catchy leaflets telling me about factory close-outs, final liquidations, about going-out-of-business sales, mean something clear about us.

But you never will go out of business, will you? It's just a new variation on your silly old offer-good-for-a-limited-time-only line, your standard order-by-midnight-tonight ploy. I've called. You know I've called. But your operators aren't standing by your tollfree number to take my call.

My last resort, and what I've always feared:

To Whom It May Concern:

It has come to my attention that I am still on your mailing list. I have tried, repeatedly, to be removed, but I keep getting this junk from you. Not even junk, just promises of junk. Shady offers. Computer generated responses: "Dear Customer, Thank you for your continued interest in our product line . . . " Don't you read my letters? Don't you understand? My mailbox is mine. You've followed me through three changes of address. I don't know where you are. How do you find me? I don't want to be on your mailing list. My mailbox is not just anybody's into which you can ram . . .

Yours truly, etc. etc.

But still it comes. Just today – an offer to subscribe to a new long distance phone call system, the Sears Vacation Wear Catalogue For People on the Go, 25 per cent off on a pair of season tickets for a theater we only went to once.

How can I express to you how desperately I want to be left alone, to be free of your recycled goods cluttering up my mailbox, my desk, my house? I don't give the Post Office my change of address card, but you're so clever you keep finding me.

I know what I'm going to do. I'm going to play your own trick back on you. I'm going to send it back to you. Though nothing you have ever sent has included your return address, I'm going to find you. On your own turf, wherever that is, the space you said you needed.

See, here I am, walking to the P.O. Can you hear me? I'm sliding gracefully into the blue tall shiny "out of town" box, resting sweetly against the soft flat backs of a hundred sleepy travellers like me.

I imagine myself a bird. I imagine myself in the belly of a plane, jostling with other packages and letters, calm sweet letters from moms to kids, tense letters from overseas lawyers. I imagine sleeping next to a dewy-eyed love letter, breathing in the perfumed scent of love.

I'll slip in through the gorgeous slim mail slot in your exquisite new apartment. I'm thin and lithe and cool and dry and sharp.

But of course I'm only dreaming that. As if I could fit into an envelope.

No, I'm afraid the only way I'll get back to you will be hard. I'll wrap myself in styrafoam peanuts, tape shut my mouth and eyes, my waiting body. I'll send me back to you, my love. I'm coming back to you.

It isn't just an ordinary box I'm in, but I don't notice this until I wake up in your tender arms again.

It's dark in here. I feel your smooth hands on my back. I'm curled inside this tiny box, tiny and crunched and bent, and you're winding me up, turning a crank in my back. And every crank you turn gets me wound tighter, waiting, busting to spring. My skin tightens, about to pop. I feel my lips pull back. This box is metal, not the soft, light, giving brown cardboard I'd crawled inside at the P.O., but tin, painted outside with garish pictures of carousels, balloons and clowns with big red noses. I'm inside this little box and that crank is cranking into me tighter and tighter, tearing through my bright red and yellow and blue and green checked nylon top, my fuzzy orange wig with the silly exaggerated bald spot, my goofy bright red lips, and two bright cheery dots of my pink cheeks. And you're still winding me tighter and tighter, and every twist you turn gets me more tense. I'm tighter, harder, smaller. My neck is arcing down into my chest. My bent arms squash into my ribs. My knees crush up against my sides. My face twists. I'm trying to scream, "Just spring me out, goddammit, let me go!" but my neck is crushed and I can hardly breathe.

Above me, outside the tin-bronze colored roof, I hear you saying words I can't understand. A chipper little circus tune tinkles along as you crank.

When the crank is wound so tight that even you can't crank it any more, when I'm so tight and doubled over, about to burst, that's when we both breathe a breath that's just alike. We hold it, then – pop! – I spew out from the lid, my arms shot apart like unconnected sleeves, little red bits of my fingers splatter like pimentos on the ceiling, my ribs cracked sideways, my torso gouged, my face split like a curtain.

This is too much even for you. You realize, at last, that you don't want this. You truly want to send me back. But who will you send me to now?

So I start getting real things in the mail. Not just the idle offers that I have been.

Boxes start arriving. I'm eager to unwrap them. I do it quickly. You've wrapped them carefully, almost lovingly. First in a plastic bag, then in tissue paper, padded with newsprint and styrafoam peanuts, all that inside a box, then wrapped with P.O.-approved paper and string. I think of you wrapping them carefully, and me unwrapping them tenderly.

But, careful as you are, the packages get tossed around, and the fragile soft insides come soaking through. I stumble to my mailbox each day in the hope that you've sent me back more. These packages contain: my hands, the soft part of my thigh, that wet red muscle hacked away from deep within my chest.

Obviously, it can't last forever.

But somehow, even after you've sent back all I thought you had of me, there's more. Where do you get this extra stuff? And how do I keep finding room for it?

I imagine my whole apartment, my entire building, packed to the ceiling with these soggy boxes. The P.O. brings them so happily, efficiently, on time. It isn't like them. They must be in with you. Now I believe, I truly believe that neither rain, nor sleet, nor snow, nor dark of night, will stop them or stop you.

There's just one way to get away. Further away than the Pony Express. Further away than anything: an island.

So I see this island.

I see myself. I'm floating above it like a silent, separate eye, no form or body, hovering in the air above a tropical paradise. It's a tiny island from above, not more than a couple of miles across. It's mostly sand – harsh, brittle, bright – a hard little nut of white in the perfect sea. I see jagged shapes where the sand juts into the blue-green sea. There are lagoons of water. The island is mostly sand, but there are groups of palm trees and coconut trees, some places that must be shady. And there must be caves, cool places hidden from the sun. And maybe there's a hut I've slung together from palm branches and driftwood. And maybe there's a soft place on the ground I've cleared away beneath a tree where I can rest. Because I'm on the island. Yes, that's me. I'm the little shape I see below me, so tiny and sharp. I watch my movements and from this height, even if in fact they're smooth and calm, they all look tiny and fast, nervous and twitchy as a rodent. I can't tell what I'm trying to do from this height. I think perhaps I'm only trying to rest.

But it's so hard to tell from here. I don't want to leave this distant, cool blue sky, but as soon as I wonder too much what's going on down there, I get pulled down. I can't help it.

So here I am, this is how it looks from here. I'm on the island now and it's hot. It's really hot.

My bare feet are hot in the sand. I'm not sure how big this place is, but I know I'll survive. At least, though I'm still panting from my rough arrival here, I know that somehow, finally, I'll be allowed to breathe easier, both my heaving lungs intact.

I don't know what I'll eat. I've no idea what the seasons are. I look down at the bright white sand between my feet. I close my eyes. I imagine this island covered with white, the tops of palm trees poking out, their big leaves sagging under the coat of fine white powder. I imagine myself the Little Match Girl, standing on the street corner, trying to sell matches in it. No – no – I squint my eyes tighter and clench my teeth until I imagine myself skiing and graceful, my calves firm, my back strong, down monstrous alps of it. I feel cold spray on my face as I whup the skis beside me with my confident, sure hands. My throat feels cool. But when I start to swallow, I choke.

I snap my eyes open and blink. I slap my cheeks. I'm hot, really hot. There's sweat on my eyes. I stretch up slowly, an effort, and walk the few steps to the beach, dip my hands in the water and bring it to my face and splash. I look down at the water. It's wavy. I know there's shade somewhere on this island, I've just got to find it. I cup my hands in the water again and bring them to my mouth and drink. I squat by the water and look for signs of fish or mussels or something green and living. But the water is perfectly clear. My stomach growls. I dip my hands in again, press them flat, fingers spread against the soft floor of the water. My wrists make pretty circles in the water. I watch the circles circle out into the clear, flat lagoon. Across the lagoon from me, a hundred yards to my left, I see the water in the rings suck down, the valleys of waves, then roll up again and crash, huge now, against both sides of the lagoon I'm at the apex of. I pull my hands out of the water and squat further back on the ground, my innocent hands limp at my sides. I look at the ocean in front of me. It's choppy now, frothy whitecaps slapping each other. The insides of the waves are pressed down hard like air is pushing them.

I look up when I hear the sound. Above me in the air above my island, a helicopter, its huge propeller spinning perfectly, slicing the air in two. It's pressing the water beneath its invisible thumb.

I see the glint of the sun on the round, insect eye of the helicopter window. I see the competent, round feet spin in the air below the belly. I see the gentle sway of its tail, sassy and suggestive.

I stand and lift my hands above my head. I wave, suddenly joyful and frantic at once, hopeful and eager and ready. I think I see a waving back. Yes − a sure hand from the window. The sun glints harsh against the window of the helicopter, and hard against my eyes. I close my eyes and can imagine so clearly the dropping of the rope ladder to me, its manic twisting in the air. I imagine the gaping door waiting for me to rise to it. I look up, shielding my face from the sun with my hand. The sun is brilliant on the helicopter shell; no rope's been thrown to me.

I wave again now, fast and worried. This takes most of my waning strength. Then I'm practically jumping up and down, panting, waving, eager and inviting and believing. My head is hot. My eyes are wet. I close my eyes and try to catch my breath. My chest is heaving.

When I open my eyes, I see it falling. A tiny fleck through the ungiving air. Then bigger. It's brown and square and not attached to anything. It spins down like a falling leaf towards me.

A package. It lands with a thud. I see the soft poof of sand that rises when it hits. I stumble over and kneel down beside it; brown wrapping paper, bound with string and tape. I turn it right-side-up. Some of the tape has popped. Some of the corners have been crushed with the fall, but I push them gently to smooth the rumpled paper. I brush the sand off and read the address: my name.

I grab the box in both arms and hug it to my chest. I fall back into the burning sand. I look back up to the burning sky. Is what I see the glint of sun, or the pink shape of a hand inside the window?

I know it's you, my darling, this package is from you. You're hand-delivering back the parts of me to me.

I see your pink hand moving in the window. Are you waving to me, my love? Have you come to say hello or ask forgiveness?

No – it's not a wave. Just you pushing another speck out the door. I watch it spinning in the air, a pin prick in an arc of sky. I see it grow, another block in beige, Post Office-approved wrapping paper. I run, still clutching the first package in my arms, to where I think the second will land. I hold my free arm out to it as if I'll break its fall, but I'm not fast enough, or skilled. It thumps the sand. I trip and fall and grab it in my arms. My mouth and eyes are full of sand. I see my name you've written on the label. I see the corner seam that's red and wilted, part of me inside. I squeeze the boxes in my arms and throw my head back far. I look up at the sky and up at you. I hear the humming quiet down. I see your harsh propeller pull away from me.

I drop the unopened packages in the sand and leap up flinging both my tired arms. I shout to you, bend down to snatch the packages. I jerk my head back and forth between you and the boxes I'm trying to open. I don't know if you're coming back. I know what's in the packages.

I try to put them out of sight, in hidden places – dark interiors of caves, and under rocks, and off the paths I travel on my rounds to water, food and rest. But soon I can't. Soon I'm stacking them in piles. There isn't room.

You come all the time and drop them always. More and more of them. I don't have time to open them, no time to wave to you. I scurry back and forth trying to stack the new ones in the ever greater piles.

They've filled the woods. It's not a question anymore of keeping them out of sight, but of hacking a path between them. They're underneath my feet, tight and hard and firm as bricks. They're high as my chest, my throat. I climb up stacks of them to put more on top.

They come so suddenly, so fast, I don't have time to make a plan. But somewhere in the back of my mind, dear love, yes, somewhere in the bottom of my heart, I tell myself, I know, that someday, darling, all this will be yours, yes, someday this will reach you, darling, all of this will add back up to you, a pile so high you'll ram back into it, your fine propeller mangling against the dense and pressing packages you have returned to me.

But I don't have time to think this. You never let me rest. I never stop. And even when I do, I don't know when I will. I just keep stacking boxes up. They keep arriving, constant, steady, always a surprise, day after day, each hour, every time I blink or try to breathe, just when I think I know they will, just when I think you've sent me back, just when I think there can't be any more, when I think you'll do this to me forever, when I think, just when I think –

FORGIVENESS

WHEN I SAID I'D give my right arm for you, I didn't think you'd ask me for it, but you did.

You said, Give it to me.

And I said OK.

There were lots of reasons I gave it to you.

First of all, I didn't want to be made a liar of. (I had never lied to you.) So when you reminded me that I'd said it and asked me if I really meant it, I didn't want to seem like I was copping out by saying that I'd only spoken figuratively. (It is an old saying, after all.) Also, I had the feeling you didn't think I would really do it, that you were testing me to see if I would, and I wanted you to know I would.

Also, I believed you wouldn't have asked me for it unless you really wanted it, and needed it.

But then, when you got it, you bronzed it and put it on the mantel over the fireplace in the den.

The night you took it, I dreamt of arms. I slept on the couch in the den because I was still bleeding, even through the bandages, and I knew I'd stir during the night and need to put on more bandages and we didn't want me to wake you up. So I stayed on the couch and when I slept, I dreamt of arms: red arms, blue arms, golden arms. And arms made out of jade. Arms with tattoos, arms with stripes. Arms waving, sleeping, holding. Arms that rested up against my ribs.

We kept my arm in the bathtub, bleeding like a fish. When I went to bed, the water was the color of rose water, with thick red lines like strings. And when I woke up the first time to change my bandages, it was colored like salmon. Then it was carnation red, and then maroon, then burgundy, then purple, thick, and almost black by morning.

In the morning, you took it out. I watched you pat it dry with my favorite big fat terry cloth towel and wrap it in saran wrap and take it out to get it bronzed.

I learned to do things differently. To button my shirts, to screw and unscrew the toothpaste cap, to tie my shoes. We didn't think of this. Together, we were valiant, brave and stoic. Though I couldn't quite keep up with you at tennis anymore.

In a way, it was fun. Things I once took for granted became significant. Cutting a steak with a knife and fork, or buttoning my fly, untying a knot around a bag, adding milk while stirring.

After a while, I developed a scab and you let me come back to bed. But sometimes in the night, I'd shift or have a nightmare, jolt, and suddenly, I'd open up again, and bleed all over uncontrollably. The first time this happened neither of us could go back to sleep. But after a while, you got used to it and you'd be back asleep in a minute. It didn't seem to bother you at all.

But I guess after a while it started bothering you, because one day when I was washing out the sheets I'd bloodied the night before, you said, You sleep too restless. I don't like it when your bleeding wakes me up. I think you're sick. I think it's sick to cut off your own arm.

I looked at you, your sweet brown eyes, innocent as a puppy. But you cut it off, I said. You did it. You didn't blink. You asked me for it, so I said OK.

Don't try to make me feel guilty, you said, your pretty brown eyes looking at me. It was your arm.

You didn't blink.

I closed my eyes.

That night I bled again. I woke up and the bed was red, all full of blood and wet. I reached over to touch you and to wake you up and tell you I was sorry, but you were not there.

I learned more. To cook and clean, to eat a quarter pounder with one fist, to balance my groceries on my knee while my hand fumbled with the front door key.

My arm got strong. My left sleeve on my shirts got tight and pinched. My right shirt sleeve was lithe and open, carefree, like a pretty girl.

But then the novelty wore off. I had to convince myself. I read about those valiant cases, one-legged heroes who run across the continent to raise money for causes, and paraplegic mothers of four, one-eyed pool sharks. I wanted these stories to inspire me, but they didn't. I didn't want to be like those people. I didn't want to be cheery and valiant. I didn't want to have to rise above my situation. What I wanted was my arm.

Because I missed it. I missed everything about it. I missed the long solid weight of it in my sleeve. I missed clapping and waving and putting my hand in my pocket. I missed waking up at night with it twisted behind my head, asleep and heavy and tingling.

And then I realized that I had missed these things all along, the whole time my arm had been over the mantel, but that I'd never said anything or even let myself feel anything bad because I didn't want to dwell on those feelings because I didn't want to make you feel bad and I didn't want you to think I wanted you to feel bad.

I decided to look for it. Maybe you'd sold it. You were always good with things like that.

I hit the pawnshops. I walked into them and they'd ask me could they help me and I'd say, I'm looking for an arm. And they'd stare at me, my empty sleeve pinned to my shirt, or flapping in the air. I never have liked acting like things aren't the way they are.

When I searched all the local pawnshops, I started going to ones further away. I saw a lot of the country. It was nice. And I got good at it. The more I did, the more I learned to do. The braver ones would look at me directly in the eye. They'd give me the names and addresses of outlets selling artificial limbs, or reconstructive surgeons. But I didn't want another one, I wanted mine. And then, the more I looked for it, the more I wondered if I wasn't looking more for something else besides my severed arm. I wondered was I really searching for you?

It all came clear to me. Like something hacked away from me; you'd done this to me as a test. To show me things. To show me what things meant to me, how much my arm was part of me, but how I could learn to live without it. How, if I was forced to, I could learn to get by with only part of me, with next to nothing. You'd done this to me to teach me something.

And then I thought how, if you were testing me, you must be watching me, to see if I was passing.

So I started acting out my life for you. And then I felt you watching all my actions. I whistled with bravado, jaunted, rather than walked. I had a confident swagger. I slapped friendly pawnshop keepers on their shoulders and told them jokes. I was fun, an inspiration they'd remember after I'd passed through.

I acted like I couldn't care less about my old arm. Like I liked the breezes in my sleeve.

I began to think in perfect sentences, as if you were listening to me. I thought clear sentences inside myself. I said, I get along just fine without my arm. I think that I convinced myself, in trying to convince you, that I had never had an arm I'd lost.

Soon I didn't think the word inside me any more. I didn't think about the right hand gloves buried in my bottom drawer.

I made myself not miss it. I tested myself. I sat in the den and stared at the empty space above the mantel. I spent the night on the couch. I went into the bathroom and looked in the tub. I felt nothing. I went to bed.

I thought my trips to pawnshops, my wanderlust, were only things I did to pass the time. I thought of nothing almost happily.

I looked at my shoulder. The tissue was smooth. I ran my fingers over it. Round and slightly puffed, pink and shiny and slick. As soft as pimento, as cool as a spoon, the tenderest flesh of my body.

My beautiful empty sleeve and I were friends, like intimates.

So everything was fine.

For a while.

Then you came back.

Then everything did.

But I was careful. It had been a long time. I had learned how to live. Why, hadn't I just forgotten what used to fill my empty sleeve entirely? I was very careful. I acted like nothing had ever been different, that you had never ripped it out of me, then bronzed it, put it on the mantel, left with it. I wanted things to stay forgot.

And besides, it was so easy, so familiar having you around. It was nice.

I determined to hold on to what I'd learned. About the strength of having only one.

Maybe I should have told you then. Maybe I should have told you then. But then, I told myself, if you knew to leave it alone, then good. And if you didn't know, we needed to find that out.

So we were sitting in the den. You looked at me with your big sweet pretty brown eyes and you said, you whispered it softly like a little girl, you said, Oh, I'm so sorry. You started crying softly, your lips quivering. Can you ever forgive me? You said it slow and sweet like a foreign language. I watched you, knowing you knew the way I was watching you. You leaned into me and pulled my arm around you and ran your pretty fingers down the solid muscle in my sleeve. Just hold me, darling, you said. Just hold me again.

I ran my wet palm, shaking, on your gorgeous back. Your hair smelled sweet.

I looked at your beautiful tear-lined face and tried to pretend that I had never seen you before in my life.

Why did you do it? I whispered.

You looked at me, your eyes all moist and sweet like you could melt anything in the world. You didn't answer.

What did you do with it?

You shrugged your shoulders, shook your head and smiled at me sweeter than an angel.

Say something, I whispered into your pretty hair. Say something, goddammit.

You looked up at me and your sweet brown eyes welled up with tears again. You put your head against my breast and sobbed.

You made me rock you and I did and then you cried yourself to sleep as innocent as a baby. When you were asleep I walked you to the bedroom and put you to bed. You slept. I watched you all night. You remembered nothing in the morning.

In the morning we had coffee. You chatted to me about your adventures. You cocked your head at just the right places, the way I remembered you did. You told me you'd worked hard in the time you'd been away. You told me you had grown. You told me how much you had learned about the world, about yourself, about honor, faith and trust, etc. You looked deep into my eyes and said, I've changed. You said how good and strong and true and truly different you were. How you had learned that it is not our acts, but our intents, that make us who we are.

I watched your perfect teeth.

I felt your sweet familiar hands run up my body, over the empty sleeve that rumpled on the exposed side of me. I closed my eyes and couldn't open them. My mouth was closed. I couldn't tell you anything.

I couldn't tell you that you can't re-do a thing that's been undone. I couldn't tell you anything that you would understand. I couldn't tell you that it wasn't just the fact that you had ripped it out of me and taken it and mounted it, then left with it then lost it, how it wasn't only that, but it was more. How it was that when you asked me, I believed you and I told you yes. How, though I had tried a long time to replace what you had hacked away from me, I never could undo the action of your doing so, that I had, and only ever would have, more belief in your faulty memory, your stupid sloppy foresight, than in your claims of change. How I believed, yes, I believed with all my heart, that given time, you'd do something else again, some new and novel variant to what you'd done to me, again. And then I thought, but this was only half a thought, that even if you had changed, no *really* changed, truly and at last, and even if you knew me better than I know myself, and even if I'm better off than I've ever been, and even if this was the only way we could have gotten to this special place where we are now, and even if there's a reason, darling, something bigger than both of us, and even if all these even if's are true, that I would never believe you again, never forget what I know of you, never forget what you've done to me, what you will do, I'll never believe the myth of forgiveness between us.

LADY BOUNTIFUL AND THE
UNDERGROUND RESISTANCE

THERE WAS A KNOCKING at the door.

No one who belonged here knocked. And no one who did not belong came out here anymore. And no one could be lost. The lines were drawn, the gate was clear and marked. Everybody knew where they belonged.

There was only one person who would have knocked.

Who is it? I asked, my voice quivering like a grandma in her nightie.

I heard a throat clearing, an uncomfortable shifting of feet, a clicking away of shoes. But no answer.

You didn't know who to say you were.

There was a knocking at the door.

Who is it?

You cleared your throat, It's me.

Who? I asked, as if poor old grandma me was hard of hearing.

It's — it's Lady Bountiful.

I paused like any hard-of-hearing, harmless old maid would. Lady Who? as if I'd never heard the name before.

Lady Bountiful, you enunciated haughtily.

I'm sorry, I don't know anyone by that name, I lied.

Everybody knew that name, that name was in the paper and on the porticoes of the renovated buildings and at the new convention center. Everybody knew how you had swept Lord Bountiful off his big, black-booted feet.

I heard you hesitate. Then leave.

This was a mere formality, a *petite pas de deux,* your knocking, my not opening. Everybody knew each crummy dump and cubby hole and puny shack and rotten hut and dinky garret around was owned by Lord Bountiful. He kept his working girls in them. You could have, by asking him, had the horseguards trample down my door.

Yet you continued knocking. You couldn't let Lord Bountiful know you came. You were forbidden here, and yet you came. In a way it amused and somewhat comforted me to realize we had not been unique in being the object of your deceptions.

You came at night. You couldn't be seen at this dirty, low-life underside of a place. But you knew where it was. You used to live here.

There was a knocking at the door.

I was waiting.

Who is it?

It's me, you whispered.

Who?

It's — You whispered the old name I used to know you by.

She isn't here anymore, I said, my voice quivering like a poor old maid.

No, you interrupted me, I'm not here for her, I am her.

No you're not.

But you were desperate to persuade me.

There was a knocking at the door. Very lightly this time, like a co-conspirator. You used your stage whisper, Pssst! It's me! Lemme in you guys!

You didn't know what had happened to our old gang. At first I was angry at your ignorance: how could you be so unaware of what had been so earth-shattering to us? But then I was glad: if you thought you were dealing with the gang, rather than just me, you might act a little better.

Lemme in you guys! It's me!

I was leaning against the inside of the door. I felt the hard, ungiving firmness of your body on the other side. I wondered if you felt me too. You couldn't see me but I saw you through the tiny crack that appeared in the door when you left.

I'd shut the lights off in the hut, it was completely dark inside. Outside the night was dark, but behind you, way back up the alley, waiting for you, was a skinny, barefoot urchin girl. She was holding an official-issue flashlight and a bag. The beam of light was greenish white. Her skin shone orange and the muscles in her arms were tight from where she held the bag. Very close to me, not six inches away, I saw the side of your face pressed against the door. Your hands were flat against the door as if you thought your touch, like some old charm, could open it.

You were wearing the ragged overalls you wore the night you left. Though you couldn't see me watching you, you knew I did. You tugged at the bib of your overalls as if I'd think, because you wore the uniform, you were still one of us. Also, as a special trick for me, you'd smudged your hands with something blue. Your lips and tongue were also blue. When you had planned this scene, you'd planned to get inside and have me see you thus, thereby distracting me so I wouldn't see your urchin drop the bag inside the hut, beside the mat, from whence it came.

You wore these things to remind me of something you used to do when you were working. You'd forget there was ink on your hands and when we heard the horses we'd all be terrified and turn the equipment off and pile things up by the door and throw ourselves behind the printer and the stacks and pray. We were all afraid. You bit your nails. This made your lips and tongue turn blue. And sometimes later, from comforting you, I got this blueness on me too. So that was why, this night when you came back to me, you'd made yourself look like that, to trick me. But I wasn't going to fall for it. Through the crack in the door I also saw your fingernails – long and round and soft-looking and smooth. The manicure you took for granted now gave you away.

Pssst! Lemme in you guys! It's me!

When you didn't hear anything inside you gestured to the girl who held your flashlight and the bag. The girl approached. I saw her light bob down the alley. She shone the light directly on the door. You looked at the door to see if there were any signs of life. When you became convinced the place was empty and were about to turn away, I surprised you.

Are you alone? My voice was hoarse.

You gasped. This wasn't the first time I'd surprised you when you were not alone. You put your finger to your lips to silence the girl. I smiled at how alike yourself you still were. You'd never been good at this question. From the way you bit your lower lip, I saw you realized how obvious was your tired old lie.

Come back alone, I whispered.

You hesitated. You put your finger to your lips again to keep the flashlight urchin quiet. Your feet shuffled. When I heard the clicking of your shoes, I clicked the camera. When the girl was a few yards from the door, she turned and looked back at the door, right at the crack, and winked.

One of your duties as First Lady was to allow your wonderful name to be associated, as gracious patroness or generous benefactress, with a social issue – i.e. some unimportant pseudo-cause suitable to the limited scope of the fairer sex. The ideas suggested to you included such deserving projects as the Adopt a Girl at the Zoo project, and the Plant a Tree project and the Tiles in the Market Place project, all schemes which certainly required the feminine touch. You chose the Plight of the Poor Unfortunates Project. You were to do things like have your photo taken standing next to the Harvest Festival turkey which Lord Bountiful was generously donating to the poor unfortunates (that is—us) out of the goodness of his heart. Though the bald fat bird you posed beside was barely big enough to make soup for a hundredth of us, the shot went over well on the front page of the recently launched *Bountiful Times.* You were wearing a particularly festive pillbox hat.

You threw lavish receptions in which you pretended to coax (pre-arranged) agreements from fat cat grain and vegetable dealers to put aside for us poor unfortunate working girls the stuff so rotten they would otherwise have thrown it out. You performed these staged and scripted acts of kindness well.

But then a rumor started. Word got around that you were taking what was meant to be merely a symbolic, superficial interest in a public relations ploy, seriously. Instead of merely cutting ribbons and popping bottles of champagne and smiling your perfect, recently capped, smile for the cameras, it was suggested that you were actually having contact – *personal* contact – with the poor unfortunates.

You were. You were coming to me.

In exchange for a little light typing, the flashlight girl saw to it that the rumors reached the press. There was even a rumor of a photograph.

So one morning when Lord Bountiful was dragging home a cartful of game from a Big Boys Club safari, an off-beat boy reporter from *Bountiful Times* flapped a photo in front of him and asked, Is there any truth to the rumor that Lady Bountiful is stepping out?

Lord Bountiful answered with his riding crop. None whatsoever, boy, and it would behoove you not to spread such trash.

The boy had little chance thereafter to; by the time he returned to the office he had been demoted to the mailroom.

That night, back in your chamber, Lord Bountiful flung you down on your big white canopied princess bed.

Just what the hell is this about?

You didn't know how to deny it. Suddenly you remembered what you had tried to ignore last time you left me – the sound of the camera's click. You'd hoped your ragged overalls would mask your true identity and let you pass for any nameless working girl, but your pretty, manicured white hands raised up to shush the flashlight girl gave you away.

And that's what Lord B pointed at, the photo of your soft, white, well-acquainted hands. How white they looked beside your blue-black mouth! You couldn't deny the shot was you. Lord B couldn't see the setting, but seeing you dressed like us was enough to make him wonder not only about the motives of your project, but also about the secret of your past.

He grabbed you by your shoulders. His fingertips were very close to the purple, petal-sized marks on your neck. He moved his hand along your throat.

What on god's green ass have you been up to?

A charity project, you choked.

Like hell.

Lord Bountiful wasn't dumb. He kept his fingers on your neck for several seconds while you shook.

But, to tell the truth, he didn't rough you up. Not the way, if I were him, if I were as big as him and if I knew what I know about you now, I would. I'd slap your lying mouth and knock you down and kick your tits and your fucking ass and then, but only then, I'd say, as Lord Bountiful said then, You go there again I'll break your neck.

In a way I admire Lord Bountiful. Not only his power. Not only that he has made me what I am to some degree (regard my lungs, the shape of me). I not only respect, I positively appreciate him. I like how clear he is. Unlike yourself, Lady Bountiful, he doesn't hem and haw. He isn't coy, does not say one thing when he means another. He states demands and tells how he will get. He doesn't backtrack or prevaricate. He marches in and he announces, "Mine." He doesn't offer false condolences. He never pretends to be sincere when he is not. He never uses lines like, "This hurts me more than it hurts you," "I'm sorry it has to be like this," "Someday you'll understand," "Someday." On the contrary, he speaks directly: "You." "Out." And if he feels like explaining, though he very rarely does, the reason he gives is: "This is the way I want it." And it is.

You swear to yourself you won't get caught. You swear this time will be your last. You swear you'll do it this time then you'll never ever ever come back again. But you come back. You keep coming back. There's something you need to get rid of. You want me to take it. You tell me it's mine, you tell me it's a gift. But I know each gift you give is not a gift. Your acts of love are only acts. You play pretend. What you made with your body was not love, it was a lie. Each gift of yours is a demand, a poor attempt to bribe your way away from what you've done. Each gift you want to give is an excuse, a toy, a bauble in lieu of something irreplaceable. You're trying to pay an unpayable debt. You're trying to buy forgiveness.

There was a knocking at the door.

Who is it? My voice was like a shy old maid.

Hello-o-o! you sang. You were trying to sound chipper, as if this was the first time you had come here, as if this old charade was fresh and new and I would let you in. Then, like a rich, smart auntie from the city to your secret country bastard, you said, I've brought you something!

I was leaning against the inside of the door. I looked through the crack. It was raining, but the girl who was holding the umbrella over your head was doing such a good job you weren't even damp. It was actually more of a parasol, pink, with fringe around the edges. This told me more about what you'd become than I wanted to know. I cringed. The pastel dress you wore was fresh and crisp. You looked like a hairspray ad.

You were smiling your sweet full-of-pity-for-the-poor-unfortunates smile as if you really were here on an official First Lady charity visit. But of course it was the middle of the night.

I have something for you, you said.

Though you couldn't see me, you knew I was watching. You acted out this scene for me. You lowered your eyelids and bowed your head and then, because the umbrella girl missed these cues, you snapped your fingers at her. She hoisted the bag up to the door, loosened her hand and let the bag fall open.

What is it? I rasped through the door.

Open the door. Your voice was carefully modulated. Look, look you silly girl, Look in the bag.

But I wouldn't look. I wanted you to say it.

And then, as if you thought you hadn't played your part with enough gusto, you lowered your head and fluttered your eyelashes and spread your arms in a benevolent benediction and said, a little louder, For you.

No! I shouted to mask the sound of the camera's click as I shot you and the bag.

Pardon me? You sputtered with surprise. They hadn't taught you how to deal with the ungrateful poor unfortunates.

No. I don't want it.

But it's for you. You whispered as if you were being sensitive about a difficult, embarrassing topic, Aren't you hungry?

I didn't answer.

There was only the sound of the rain. Then in a couple of seconds there was creaking. You still weren't used to those pinchy, pointy little shoes they made you wear. But then you had a bright idea.

I'll leave it outside your door! you chirped, Just here, all right? You can come out and get it after we're gone if you're shy!

You were so pleased with yourself for coming up with this clever solution. Bye-bye! You sounded perky.

You slapped your hands together as if to say, That's taken care of.

But it wasn't.

After the girl and you were gone, I turned on all the lights in the hut. I ripped the polaroid out of the camera, flapped it in the air and lay it on the table to dry. I plugged the xerox in and hit the button. The machine coughed a bit, but when I kicked it, it started to hum. I tore open a fresh packet of 8½ x 11, flipped the paper through my fingers to make sure none of the pages were bent, and loaded the paper tray. On the old Sears manual we'd appropriated from Shipping and Receiving, I typed. The tips of my four fingers were grimy when I finished typing the words. By the time I tore the paper out of the typewriter, the copier Ready button was green. I lifted the lid and lay the message face down against the glass. I punched the magnify button, then Print. I was so eager to see the words I hadn't heard for so long I had to force myself to not grab the paper when it started to squeeze out the other side. I watched the edge of the white-grey paper widen, then the letters came from the machine. They were lovely.

I lifted the warm, limp copy from the tray. It bent in the air like a languid, used-up girl. I opened the lid again and lay it face down. I pressed my palm to its backside to move it where I wanted it. Then I shut the cover over it. I did this several times – oh I could have done it forever! – each time more heady, each time more full of the excitement of the getting-bigger words. When the words were as big as I wanted them, I drew next to them a cartoon stick figure of a skinny, bony, starving, mutilated, yet grotesquely smiling, perhaps retarded, working girl. Next to this drawing I taped the polaroid of you. I lay the page with drawing, words and polaroid in collage, down on the glass. The glass was still warm. When I lay the flexible, soft, thick rubber sheet of the lid down on the page, I felt like I was tucking someone into bed. I patted the cover down and held my hand on it a moment to prolong the sweetness of the moment before I whacked the button. I whacked the button. I squatted at the end of the machine. Heat came out of the open slit. Inside I saw that snap of green-white light that meant it was getting it. I heard the clicking and groaning as the paper started to move. The hot white printed edge of the page started poking out. The paper made a sssshhh sound as it pushed through, like it was saying Yesss. The blank edge of the border came out first, then the exclamation points, then–the far right of the polaroid – your hands held out in benediction – then, above and below the photo, the letters. First U, then 0, then Y. My heart was beating fast. I was so happy! So happy! I was shot through with happiness! Oh would it would never end! It was so beautiful! I hit the counter for 99 and let her rip.

The flyers that appeared the next day were of you and that scrawny cartoon girl. The words on the poster were short and sweet. They said. THANK YOU! ! ! I LOVE YOU! ! !

Even the horseguards, who were not among the most clever of God's creatures, understood. And of course, Lord B, who did in fact have quite a brain to match his mighty brawn, knew what it meant.

There was a desperate pounding at the door.

Before I could say, Who is it? you were hissing, What the hell have you done? Why did you do what you did?

To thank you, I said, as quiet and as righteous as a priest on this side of the door of your confession.

You've got to take it back. You've got to undo it.

Nothing can be undone, I counselled wisely.

Everybody in the city has seen what you've done!

What I've done? No, Lady B, what you've done. All I've done is make it known.

I didn't want anyone to know.

You didn't want anyone to know you'd come tonight; you hadn't even brought your flashlight girl.

Don't hide your light under a bushel, Lady B, I exhorted. And surely you remember, after all, that what we're here for in this hut, is to tell the tale.

What I brought was a special gift, a private gift for you.

To call a thing a private thing was one of your favorite methods of denial.

I heard you plop down on the ground and cry.

Do you know what will happen to me if he figures out I come here?

Yes, I answered. Also like a Father, I know everything.

I wouldn't have brought it back if I thought you'd tell, you pouted.

Well . . .

Through the crack in the door I saw you lift your head because you thought you detected some crack in my resolve.

No one will find it here.

You sighed in relief.

I've sent it back to you.

What! You leapt up.

In exchange for letting her use the xerox to make some trendy collage stationery, the flashlight and umbrella girl had not only agreed to help me put the flyers up all over town, the way the old gang used to do, but also to drag the bag back to your place.

But I don't want it now.

You wanted it enough to steal it once, I snapped. I didn't sound like your Daddy anymore.

I can't keep it, you mumbled.

You should have thought of that before.

You never thought of anything before.

You ran home as fast as your ridiculous little shoes would carry you. You found it where you knew I'd have left it – your bed. You dragged it out. You couldn't leave it where so many different people could come across it. You had to hide it where no one could get it without your knowing. You hid it on your person. You tied it to your body underneath your skirts.

I saw you pick it up and press the sturdy, leather-like material next to your skin and I saw you tie the cord that tied the top of it together to your body. I saw you suck your gut in to accommodate the bulk and I saw your trembling lower lip as you were thinking how unfair, how unkind of me to not allow it back. I saw you tie the knot around yourself and pull it tight. I saw you think that if you held it close to you, as close as skin, no one would see. I saw you turn and preen before the mirrors in your room so you'd discover which positions hid it best. I saw you bite your nails when you wondered how you'd hide it from Lord B. Then shake your head and exhale quickly as you remembered how single-minded and otherwise unaware he was when you performed your duties: he probably wouldn't notice what you removed from underneath your skirt as long as you removed it quickly. I saw you press it and try to shape it to fit the contours of your body. And though you hid it well still it was heavy.

When you first left I dreamt you would come back. I dreamt and I imagined, every day and every night when I was herded down to work, that you'd come back. I dreamt that you had not done what you'd done. Or then I dreamt that you had done it, but had changed, no really, truly changed, and that your coming back was good and final. I dreamt that you returned and you were strong and true, immovable, a saint who was made pure by true repentance.

But after you stayed gone for long, when I imagined you back at the door, I saw you shamed, I saw you low and begging to be let in. The upright figure I saw in those dreams was me. I stood at the door and opened it and held my head up proudly, and when you saw the essence of the noble, heroic, unbroken spirit in me, you felt such remorse for what you'd done you fell down on your knees and wept. This scene continued as I leaned down to you, magnanimous and saintly, and I, of all us poor, unfortunate and horribly mistreated girls, held out my holy hand to you and took the bag you'd crawled back with and let you in.

But that's what I dreamt long ago.

You came to me at night. I worked the day shift. Not that it mattered. The hours we worked, whether night or day, meant we were waking up in the dark and returning home after dark again. When it was time for our shift we were summoned by their lights and by the clattering of hooves. We leapt up from our mats and stumbled to the ghetto gate where the horseguards herded us. They made us keep our heads bowed low as they corralled us to the mines. They sat on their horses and prodded us. They snapped their whips in the chilly air. Sometimes one of us didn't move quick enough or fell and was trampled. When we got inside the pit-head they handed us shovels and axes and ropes and bags. They packed us in the metal cage and sent us down. It was long and dark and rattly going down. There was always the fear that the cable would break and send us hurtling to the bottom of the hole. Some of us kept our eyes closed to try to snatch some sleep as we descended. I looked out at the hollow shaft while we were being sucked down. There were two guards on the elevator. They wore lights on their helmets and when they talked to one another those lights bobbed. When they stared at us the lights shone in our eyes and we saw spots of light and impossible color. By those small lights sometimes I saw the hard column around us, the shiny black seams and powdery dull grey patches, sometimes an illusion of something wet or red or moving or alive.

They stopped the cage and pushed us out into the seams. We worked in pairs; one of us dug at the earth while her partner collected the chunks. The chunks had to be solid and of a certain size, the chips and dust were useless. The partner collected the chunks in a bag and when the bag was full she carried the bag to a cart and poured the contents in the cart which went to the surface. It took years to work a seam, to gouge it out.

When the inside had been hacked away, the openings were supposed to be filled in and sealed. But some of them weren't, and sometimes when we were ascending in the cage at the end of the shift, we'd notice there were fewer of us on the way back up; some misbehaving or provocative or merely ordinary girl had been had in an abandoned seam. Though actually what was done unto the girls by guards occurred more often above than down below. And some girls, figuring their odds were better beneath the ground, chose to stay down there. And eventually, like the eyeless horses bred underground, they lost the desire, then the ability to see.

The ones of us who did come up again were escorted home in darkness by the guards. There was always the push and always the pressing of our tired, unresisting bodies against each other. The guards let us go at the ghetto gate and gave us a few minutes to scurry back to our huts. Once we were in our huts we were under curfew. We didn't have lights in our huts. The only lights were theirs. Sometimes when they were making their rounds, they'd shoot their flashlights in to make sure we weren't moving. We didn't want to move. We wanted to sleep. But every night we heard the clacking of the hooves. And sometimes in the night we'd hear stampeding. We'd hear the hooves run back and forth over the body of some broken girl who had tried to get out.

We knew what would happen if we disobeyed. On the other hand, being a good girl didn't guarantee one's safety. Sometimes, not because she'd tried to escape, but just because, they'd pick a girl. They'd drag her off her mat and out of her hut and into the street and play with her. After she collapsed they trampled her.

How different were the rest of us from those who'd stayed beneath the ground and couldn't see? It took us so long to envision that the way we'd been for so long, the way we had been told was our just lot, could change.

One day one girl threw down her shovel. She sat up and wiped the dust from her eyes and threw the chunks she'd gathered against the wall. When the chunks hit the wall and shattered to bits, the girls around her looked up in shock. To break a chunk was wicked and all the girls, especially her partner, were afraid.

I'm not going to do this anymore. Her voice was matter-of-fact. She stood up, brushing the black dust from her clothes. She raised her voice. You don't see those bastards down here doing this, do you? But who gets this stuff? Them. I'm not going to —

She didn't finish. A couple of guards swooped on her from behind. They threw a cover over her. As they hauled her off we heard her thrash. They don't live like this, she yelled, Look how they live, Look, Look —

We heard their boots. Her shouting stopped. We tried not to listen to what the workhorses and guards were doing to her in the abandoned seam, but neither the rattle of the carts, nor the sounds of our clawing and scraping, could drown out the noise of the hooves.

We shifted around to fill in for her. We hoped we would forget what we had witnessed. For a while we tried to think of her as crazy, an aberration. But no matter how hard we tried to make excuses for her act we couldn't convince ourselves she was wrong. On the contrary, we started whispering to one another she'd made sense.

When we were being shoved to work, we started to lift our eyes and glimpse, in the openings between the tenements, the brightness of the streets beyond. We saw convertibles and bronze skinned people having drinks beneath Cinzano umbrellas at riverside cafés. We saw a blue bright shiny river. We realized the popping sounds we'd heard from there weren't sounds of work, but champagne corks. They were having all-night parties. Even the horses on the other side weren't guarding; they were cruising. The only things they worked on were their tans. Beyond the ghetto where we worked like curs, those lazy, lying bastards led the good life.

Our whispering turned to rumbling. And when Lord Bountiful, ever-wise *padrone,* sensed an eruption brewing underground, he took preventative measures. Lord Bountiful's guards explained to us that though the plight of poor unfortunate working girls was natural, Lord Bountiful, in his enlightened mercy, would initiate reforms on our behalf. These promises appeased us until we saw they were merely cosmetic. Lord Bountiful launched *Bountiful Times,* a propaganda organ designed to educate us about how our lives were getting better under him. But the social service improvement programs the paper announced never got further than front page photo opportunities. We got pissed off.

But how could we resist? How could we fight their rifles and machine guns, their horses and money and nukes?

One evening when the elevator came to bring us up, some of us didn't go. We stayed below the ground and when the guards were escorting the day shift home, we raided the upper rooms. A couple of old girls had volunteered to divert the guards in the street. They started talking out loud and talking back. They said the things the crazy girl had. The guards responded eagerly. While these girls let themselves be trampled, we carted off a generator and a printer and a copier, and cases of paper and an old Sears manual typewriter from Shipping and Receiving. While the horse-guards ground those sacrificial girls to bits, we set up shop as the underground resistance.

We chose a particularly shabby hut at the end of a far-away alley. We worked there all night. The next day the world had suddenly turned spring. On the route to work the hitching posts and fence posts and the walls and gutters were flowering. The buds were flyers that showed our mutilated, hoof-marked dead. The breeze that rustled through the streets seemed to tell the names of who'd been had and whisper their terrible secrets. The awful spring recurred each morning after that. Each morning all the mining girls and the big-stick toting, leather-booted horseguards saw the evidence of who had disappeared beneath Lord Bountiful's regime. The news was spread so thick no one could anymore deny the truth.

Each night the underground resistance met. We snuck to the hut to record the atrocities. We xeroxed photos of the hoofed. We were not shy. We didn't mince. The few of us who dared to risk the streets all night slipped out through a back window, packs and pockets stuffed with posters and tape. Slipped thousands of copies to other huts and hung news from posts and taped it to walls and folded it into paper airplanes and flew it over the walls to the part of the city where Lord Bountiful and his fat-cat hoodlums lived.

Sometimes the girls who snuck out to take the word around did not come back. After a couple days we'd find what was left of her – her ass and mouth stuffed full, her arm cut off, her eyes gouged out, a copy of the news speared to her chest, her bloody remnants ground by horses' hooves. Sometimes they'd hang her carcass over the ghetto gate to remind us what awaited the resistance.

But each girl who was sacrificed made the rest of us more sure of our commitment. We knew that given their arms an open rebellion would be suicide, but we did the things we thought we could get away with. Our tiny acts of sabotage – the few chunks we stole home with us, the padding of the carts with dust, the pee in the cans of lighter fluid – were merely irritations to them, but they meant a lot to us. We liked seeing them made helpless by the simplest things. We liked revealing that the things they'd always called petty, not worth the bother, were in fact the things they couldn't handle. They were not only lying, lazy bastards, they were also incompetent boobs.

How could you have joined them, Lady B?

Apparently very easily.

It wasn't that you had greater things in mind. No, greater things we would have forgiven. If you had said, It's hopeless, girls, I'm jumping ship, we would have understood. If you had told us you'd come to believe we were wrong or wicked or unnatural, we would have respected your opinion. If you had said you were embarrassed. Or tired. Or if you'd admitted you just felt like a change of air. If you had told us anything at all, we would have agreed to disagree. Unlike yourself, the rest of us actually believed what we said about self-determination, right to choose, and even, heaven help our innocence, allowing one another space.

But you didn't have the decency to tell us.

I remember the night you left. I remember how slowly I reacted because I couldn't believe you were doing what you did.

All of us resistance girls were working, as we did each night, in this small hut where you and I once lived. We were all intent upon our tasks. There was so much bustle and activity we didn't notice you. You were supposed to be printing some oversize posters and stacking them on the bench next to me. (We always worked together, you and I. We knew each other's moves by heart.) I was cropping some photos. I was good at knowing what details of a picture were true and what were decoration. Only when I noticed the stack wasn't getting bigger did I see you weren't working. I was flustered; always before I had sensed when you were near and when you weren't. But the night you left, this extra sense in me broke down. I saw some movement in the corner where we kept our mat. It was you, bending over and moving as quick and evasive as a rat. You were putting something in my bag.

I was so surprised I said outloud, What are you doing?

The girls around me shushed me. We never spoke outloud. We had to avoid making any sounds that might give us away to them.

Ssssh, you joined our comrades in silencing me.

They turned back to their work and didn't watch you.

I dropped my work and hurried to you. You were filling my bag.

What are you doing? I whispered.

You hid the bag behind you.

Nothing, you lied. You were never a very creative liar.

What are you doing with my stuff? I nodded at the bag.

Your pretty brown eyes got as wide as an innocent baby's.

What are you —

The girls turned around to shush me again. You put your fingers to your lips to tell me, Ssssh.

When I was quiet you started walking to the door.

No one went out the door at night. Opening the door would let the light and noise of our machines out in the street and alert the guards.

You can't go out, I whispered.

But you kept walking. I could feel your body pulling away; the band between us was pulling tight and thin. When you put your hands up to open the door I screamed. Don't leave me!

You flung the door open and ran. I started to run after you but a girl grabbed me. She slapped her hands over my mouth. Another girl slammed the door and others cut the lights and machines. I was thrashing around in my comrade's arms.

They'll get her! I yelled.

Settle down, said a girl who held me down. If they don't find us by the commotion of the machines, they'll hear your screaming.

But what'll happen to her?

She'll be all right, they mumbled.

She's got my bag. What'll happen to my stuff?

Don't think about that now, she said. None of the others would answer me. In a few minutes they slumped back to their tables and started the printers and copiers again to get back to work. Though I kept asking what would happen to you, they wouldn't answer me.

I wanted there to be a reason for what you did. I wanted someone to tell me you were doing something right.

But no one did.

We tried hard not to think of you. But I couldn't stop worrying about what they'd do to you. I couldn't put out the picture in my mind of you, and how you'd be when they found you.

Then one day, on the way to the mines, while glancing up to see our last night's posters, I saw, in the slice of the other part of town that was visible through the crack between our tenements, sitting up on the back of a gaudy Cadillac convertible, in a shiny, strapless slinky bright red dress – you.

I couldn't believe my eyes. I believed I was mistaken. I believed I was bad for having imagined such a wicked sight. When I told the girls they shook their heads or hurried away or mumbled how I was suffering.

But a few days later, someone waiting for the last elevator load down saw, through one of the control room windows where the guards kept watch, Lord Bountiful himself. He was giving a personally guided tour of his productive mines to his special guest. His special guest wore a pillbox hat. His special guest was you.

The horrible fate I'd feared for you would have been a better fate than what you sought. I couldn't anymore deny the reason you had left. You left us without honor.

Those of us who'd been with you the night you left remembered what we'd repressed about your leaving. How brazenly, how easily you'd stolen away. The tawdry truth of what you'd done discouraged some of us. Some of us lay down in the street to await the hooves. But some who had been close to you, who'd shared the greater passion of our cause, tried to keep the fact of your defection from escaping. For a while we considered fabricating the story of a martyr's death for you, but we couldn't bring ourselves to dishonor our true martyrs by naming you among them. We hoped the memory of you, like you, would leave us easily.

But the story of what you had done, like any tale of the perverse, spread rapidly. You were the example of the riches of betrayal. Some who heard what you had done used you as proof that the efforts of the underground would never pay off. They argued that you showed that no one, surely never us, could change or diminish the power of Lord Bountiful. Others chided what they called the waste of energy on manifestoes and statements and declarations. Some began to advocate the Second Wave, the New Realism, suggesting the horseguards weren't really all that bad, we just needed to re-evaluate our interpretation of what they did. And how were we to re-interpret the beatings and the tramplings and abuse? That the guards like us, were merely fulfilling natural urges and natural divisions of labor within society. And these unnaturally brainwashed girls said we needed to stop being so strident and so obsessed with the past, and learn to accept our lot in life; i.e., they wanted us to all lie down and take it. It was hard to argue with them; they didn't consider it natural for us to argue.

But the real blow came when others started following in your defective footsteps. They said if you, who'd been a founding member of the resistance, if you who lived in the very hut where the resistance met, decided to skip off and join the other side, why shouldn't they? Why shouldn't everyone?

The few of us who stayed with the resistance didn't try to tell those fickle, flighty girls what else your leaving had required, what you'd hacked off, what you had carried away.

Lord Bountiful is erecting statues of himself all over the city. Not only in the lavish mansions where they live, but also, as part of a scheme to beautify the ghetto, right in the dry, cracked patch of dirt they now call our common yard. They've installed an audio-visual program in the elevator to work. We have to watch this show, which purports to be the history of our liberation due to Lord Bountiful's benevolence, twice a day. The story is, of course, a crock of crap. At first we few remaining die-hards froth at the outlandish claims, but after a while, we're actually rather amused by the childlike, mine's-bigger-than-yours mentality of Lord Bountiful. However, most girls are too tired, and too defeated with despair, to be critical. They just nod, glassy-eyed and mute at the degrading lies we're told about ourselves.

The statues Lord B commissions are very big. There's him charging on his noble steed. And there's him trampling someone under the feet of his noble steed.

Do you recognize the girl beneath the hooves? Can you see beyond her pulled-back lips, her wild eyes, her hand clutching out at nothing? Do you recognize, dear Lady B, whom you betrayed?

But you were never good at subtleties. I bet you won't figure out the statues he's erecting are nostalgic. They're his attempts to reassert what used to be his power. He's not a growing boy anymore, but a shrinking, slow, old man. A lot of things he used to do to show off and to prove he could, he can't do anymore. He doesn't have the appetite he used to have, and he would rather not be bothered if things can be avoided. He doesn't go prowling anymore. The pictures of himself in *Bountiful Times* are all retouched. His paunch is whited out, his jowls are tucked, his hair is given color.

I doubt you'll understand this Lady B, but as he mellows out and gets a little flabby and a little scared, I realize that he and I may not be as entirely unalike as I had thought we were, and I feel for old Lord Bountiful a kind of fondness. In short, dear Lady B, that fat old man is no longer the enemy.

You are.

In the hard old days the underground resistance would have produced a special rush edition – glossy? four-color spread? an advertising insert? – to rip the lid off the secret cover-up of Lord Bountiful's demise. But not anymore.

There is no gang of girls here anymore; there's only me.

Don't think I'm boasting. I'm not the last one left because I am more true to what we once believed than everybody else. No, not at all. In fact,

I've given up my politics. I fight no more and hope no more and I no more believe that someday all of this will change, and Truth and Justice and blah blah blah. And frankly, to have given up my girlish hopes is a relief. I don't feel guilty anymore that I'm not working hard enough. In fact, I don't work on that old junk at all these days. I've turned the printer and the xerox off, and the cover of the typewriter is thick with dust. I've heard, in fact, that this old stuff is just as obsolete as ol' yours truly. But I don't care. I'm not out to change the world anymore.

But unlike the rest of our gang, who, when they gave up their politics gave up their reason to be alive, and had no choice but to lie down in the street and wait to be trampled, I've got a reason to postpone my end. Yes, something keeps me from dropping to my wrinkly knees for those stampeding stallions: You.

Each day when I wake up, I think, today may be the day! And even if it's not the day, each day makes me more happy, and I count each day that brings me one day closer to that true Someday when you come back to me. That's why I stick around, why I haven't donated the last bits of me to the Madame Bountiful's Wax Museum of Old Revolutionaries, Glue Factory and General Emporium just yet; I'm waiting for you.

I'm ready for you now. I've finally kicked away the last of my confusion. No more do I wake up in the middle of the night suffering those unguarded moments of doubt and wonder, What if I was wrong, Perhaps it wasn't as bad, It couldn't have been as bad as all that. No, now I am quite sure, quite absolutely sure, it was. It was worse, Lady Bountiful. Now I know certainly, more truthfully than any truth I ever knew before, that every thing you ever said, each thing that ever came out of your pretty, pretty mouth was a terrible lie. Now my regard for you is pure. Now I can count, and not lose count, the days and the drops and the beats and the breaths until you hobble back to me and beg me to take back the bag and let you in.

You'll come to me so frightfully, You'll say, I made a terrible mistake, You'll say, I'm sorry, You'll say, Forgive me, You'll say, Let me in.

Like hell I will.

Some nights after we had finished printing that night's edition, and after the other girls had gone, and after the equipment was quiet, and after the hut was very dark, and after the mat was very still, in that short, hard, dark black alley of the night, you wanted me. You wanted what I did to you and how I knew your body in the dark. You wanted to do what I let you do, the way I let you in. And there, inside, you told me things. You said things I believed. You said to me to hold you, Hold me hard. And after you fell in me, but before you fell entirely, you said, Don't let me go, Don't let me go – You said things I cannot repeat, you said what I believed was true, You said, This is – You said, I'll never leave – You said, Don't let me go, Don't let me go –

I said, I won't, I never will.

You're desperate to get rid of it. You've worn it underneath your skirts where it's pressed so hard it prints against your skin. When you hear someone behind you, it makes you jump. You're twitchy when someone makes polite conversation. Even the simplest questions like, Where're you from? or What's your name? or What do you do for a living? make you tongue-tied with shame. You've tried hard to get rid of it. You've tried to throw it away or push it down the disposal or flush it down the john or run it through the meat grinder. But it remains. It stays with you. It keeps itself so close to you. Like it's inside. It carries you.

Your toting it so long has made you limp. So now when you come back to me, your urchin girl not only holds the flashlight and your parasol, she also supports you by the arm. And when you go to Lord Bountiful, each night as you're beholden to, you hide it in the clothes you drop beside the bed. You're good at aiming what you slip from so it covers it, but sometimes, especially when he doesn't want you to be thinking of other things, you hear the wind blow through the room and lift your silk gown up, exposing it, and you're afraid. When you're dismissed, when he is snoring, you slip out of bed. You slide back in your clothes, you press it close against you and you tie it hard and hope that no one sees.

When I saw the flashlight girl alone, I opened the door. It was, after all, only a door.

Hi. C'mon in.

Thanks, but I gotta run. I'm only here to deliver this.

She handed me a cream-colored envelope and waited. When I read it, I laughed out loud. Tears rolled down my cheeks. I looked up at her slender throat. Her collar bone was visible above a rip in her t-shirt.

You know what this is? I asked, wiping the tears from my eyes.

Her left cheek wrinkled when she smiled. Yep.

You had sent me an invitation to: A Ball To Celebrate The Signing of The Declaration of Dependence. You'd handwritten a personal note at the bottom of the card; "Hiya! Please feel free to bring a 'freind.' Luv t' see ya!" I noted your spelling error and the way you dotted your "i's" with big fat empty circles. It was clear you had either lost or surrendered many of your faculties.

Is she serious? I asked the flashlight girl.

She nodded. Her bangs fell over her forehead.

Jesus on water skis, I said. Does Lord Bountiful know about this?

Nope, she said out of the side of her mouth. Her lips were a dusty rose color. I wanted to see her laugh.

I widened my eyes like a bimbo and said, Gosh, I haven't been to a party in ages. And never to a ball.

She smiled with half her mouth.

I put my finger to my lips, like you, and cocked my head. But—whatever will I wear?

She laughed.

I didn't send back the RSVP, but neither did I send the girl back empty-handed. I filled her compact, soft-skinned arms with a complete set of back issues of our posters, flyers, manifestoes, declarations of independence, etc. I sent you an archive set, including some signed copies, even though you probably didn't appreciate their value. What I sent you explained, point by point, and crime by crime, and death by death, what the regime you joined is guilty of.

I'm stumbling up the broad flat marble steps of the giant, wedding-cake-white mansion. I've found the joint by tagging along behind the fancy horse-drawn coaches and dark-windowed pimp-mobiles. I've slogged behind them and the mud has splattered my faded overalls, my holey sweatshirt, my worn-out work shoes. I'm clutching, in my battered hand, a copy of our manifesto. Flyers of the DISAPPEARED bulge out of my pockets. My fingernails are broken and black with dust. I know I'm not in regulation party dress, but if those arrogant snotrags try to deny me entrance to the house, I'll shove my cream-colored invitation right up their assholes.

I'm met at the door by a coffee-cart girl wearing white apron, black dress, dark tights, sensible shoes and a small white cap which actually looks more like a doily. She opens the huge, many-panelled fake baroque door. It takes her ages to open the thing, so I give her a hand. She offers me a shawl to cover my dirty work clothes, then tries a jacket, but I don't take either. I wear my position proudly. She escorts me through the tux and gown festooned crowds. They stare at me, partly out of fear that I might be contagious, but mostly out of respect for the quiet dignity that shines forth through my humble attire. They part for me like the waves of the sea for Moses. Head held high, I march beneath the dozens of huge glistening chandeliers and by the exquisite *trompe l'œil* frescos on the gallery walls. But I don't stop to glance at this junk; I know where I'm headed.

The floor of the ballroom is marble, the ceiling is a giant dome and all around the edge of the room are small tables, each with a candelabra and a bottle or two of champagne, each with some baroness or countess or general's wife or courtesan who's managed, in a very short time indeed, to push her pudgy way up through the ranks. Each of these nouveau tarts holds her puny court with a circle of clean-shaven, uniformed, bobbing-headed boys. In the center of the room, as if they were being guided by the strings of a giant puppet master, hundreds of almost identical boy – girl couples dance. In the very center of the party, in the prettiest gown of all, attached to the handsomest young buck, is you. As I push my way through the dancers, each couple I touch stops dancing. They drop their hands, their eyes glaze over, they hang their heads in shame. Everyone's stopped dancing when I reach you. The band stops playing. But you, you princess with your dream come true, have closed your eyes and raised your sticky blue eyelids towards your beau. Your escort is a movie star pin-up look-alike. I hesitate as I try to remember who he's trying to imitate. When he sees me, he stops dancing abruptly. He gulps. He isn't holding you anymore, but you keep swaying to music no one else can hear. Your limp is barely noticeable. You only stop dancing when you feel, beneath your dancing slippers, you're stepping on the edge of his toes. You open your eyes. You see his white face, his quivering chin. You see him looking behind you. You turn. You see me.

You gasp.

Have you forgotten you invited me? Or did you only send that invitation on a whim, not dreaming I would actually show up? I know how you think, you silly bitch. I can imagine you sitting in front of your make-up mirror, because whatever you did you always liked to watch yourself doing it. I can see you put your finger to your lips as if it could help you think, and I can see you cock your head, and I can hear inside your head. I can hear you thinking how clever it is to invite me because of course I won't come because I've always hated those kinds of do's, but even if I had changed and wanted to come, you figure I won't because Whatever Will I Wear? And I see you scribbling in your little girl hand, making those big fat empty circles above the "i's" and misspelling words that any third grader should know. I can see what you did so clearly – and I wasn't even there, was I? – so why the hell can't you? You may have always liked to watch yourself, to see how pretty you can get in make-up mirrors and to see the way your body moves, but you never saw, you've never seen what you did.

And neither do you remember. You don't remember you sent me an invitation and wrote a personal note to me: " . . . bring a 'freind'!" But perhaps you'll remember when you see my friends. For here they come. They're breaking through dozens of pairs of fine French doors, they're shattering glass onto the marble floor where it sprays as pretty as, though makes more of a mess than, champagne. And they're swinging down from chandeliers and leaping off balconies and banisters and running through the long, long gallery and whooping like a jungleful of Janes. You remember the old gang, don't you dear? You recognize each one of us whom you betrayed. We look the same old way we always have, we never change. We don't keep up with fashions. Except we have changed, in one small way. We've traded in our let's-try-to-relate-to-each-other-and-give-each-other-space diplomacy for sub-machine guns, uzis and some mini-nuke units we picked up cheap at a CIA garage sale. And we're about to blow your candy-ass fairy tale to smithereens.

You open your mouth, you're about to cry. You're about to tell me – again – that I don't understand, that it isn't what it looks like, that – but this time I don't listen to your shit.

No, this time your little girl pouts and your big girl lies are drowned out by the sounds of heavy artillery. The girls in the Big Is Beautiful club are rolling in in their tanks, knocking through your *trompe l'œil* walls like they were cartoons. We open fire, the girls and I, and blast the bleeding Jesus out of this house of ill repute you've clawed your way into. I'm hugging a hunk of a machine gun to my side, and as I rat-a-tat off round after round, my body shakes. I didn't know a clip could hold so much, it doesn't even take time to catch its breath. I feel the hard metal butt pound against my chest. My teeth are clenched and my hands are wet and I'm afraid my body is going to fall, but I don't let me, I don't let me, I want to see the full effulgence. But my vision starts to blur. Then all the sounds of shots and moans and cries and people begging no-please-yes get muffled. I'm not sure what happens next.

Do I find that handy rope around your middle and do I tie you up with it and make you watch us tear apart each inch of this nasty pleasure playhouse where you live? Or do we not do you the honor of singling you out for attention, but merely splatter your innards against the rococo replica furniture with everybody else's? Or do we allow you, only you of all your patten leather cohorts, to survive this spree? And do we then drag you back on your belly to where you used to live with us? Do we then make you kneel down on your skinned-up knees and do you beg us to take you back and let you be a girl like us again? Do we not let you? Or do we leave you at your house, and after we've eaten all the dip and drunk all the booze and after we've turned everything into a holocaustal wreck, say, Thanks for the fête! So long! and find our coats and our own ways to the door and leave you surrounded by overturned ashtrays and spilt drinks and torn up panties and crushed potato chips and wodges of skin and blood and peanuts ground into the carpet, and do we leave you to wonder how ever, oh how ever will you clean up this mess alone?

I don't know what we do because of course I don't go to your silly party. Not even in my maddest, my most lucid, most inspired moments do I let myself consider accepting anything you offer me. Even something as paltry and as much a sham as your offensive invitation. I know that any acceptance I would make of anything from you would give you enough to let you think I'm giving in to you. You need to think I'm giving in. You need to think I'm beginning to think how I've been towards you has been excessive. You want to think I'm going soft inside and thinking you weren't as bad as I said you were. But you were, Lady B, you were revolting. You were terrible. Your were not forgivable.

OK, maybe in my own small way, I'm as bad as you. Maybe it's just as bad to be unforgiving as it is to do something unforgivable. Maybe it's worse. Maybe you ought to be let off easy for merely being a weakling and a liar and an opportunist and a traitor and not very smart. Whereas, I know what I'm doing. I know exactly.

Perhaps if I were still the good girl trooper I once was, I'd put aside my personal feelings and consider the larger issues. Maybe I should, but I'm not going to, Lady B. Not now, especially not now, when I know what the gift you want to give me is.

Tonight you're in your party dress. It is the prettiest, the most extravagant dress, the dress that shows you finally are what you have always longed to be: the belle of the ball. The dress was very expensive and the sturdy red threads in the seams no one can see cost someone dear. But you, who've never been good with figures, haven't bothered your pretty head with learning the price of your party dress. Your dress is shiny, it dazzles so bright no one notices the hint of a limp in your dance step. And no one sees the lump beneath your skirt.

You're dancing now. Your mouth is open and laughing and you carefully pant as you glance up at your handsome partner. Your dance card is full. Another of your duties as Lady Bountiful is to entertain the troops. So all the up-and-coming officers and all the old and honored statesmen get a turn with you. You press yourself in their arms like you were everybody's one and only. You're pressed to one of these officers when you feel a tap on your shoulder. At first you think it's this booted hunk making an advance. You giggle and make yourself blush and then, a well-practiced coquette, you halfway cover your face with your fan and, with calculated ineffectiveness, pretend to push him away. You feel the tap behind you again. It isn't him. It's someone behind you. You turn. You stop smiling. It's a coffee-cart girl. You've always hated these lowly girls who've been brought up from the mines. You snarl at her. But you remember your manners quickly enough to flutter your thick blue eyelashes at your officer, Oh do excuse me.

What the hell do you want, you snarl at the girl.

Lord Bountiful would like a word with you, Ma'am. She nods curtly.

Oh do excuse me, dahling, you wink suggestively to your date, When Lord Bountiful wants me, I can't say no.

You put a good two feet between yourself and the coffee girl and twitter off. You try to sail gracefully from the ballroom, hoping the chandeliers you move beneath will nicely set off the diamonds in your tiara. You nod at the courtiers and sycophants who wisely avoid looking down at your limp. The only one who doesn't return your plastic smile is the surly, square-jawed coffee-cart girl. She follows you through the palace, past the side rooms where the canapés and duck and salmon and caviar finger sandwiches are laid. You're starting to sweat, you want to rest, but the coffee girl says, Move it.

You hobble past the card rooms and the billiard rooms and the library which contains all – and only – the back issues of *Bountiful Times*. You heave yourself up the stairs and through the galleries of the private quarters where Lord B likes to have you. At the end of the hall, where you have never been before, you stop. You don't know where to go. You hate having to exchange words with the girl, but you ask her, So where the hell am I supposed to go now?

She jerks her thumb up the skinny grey stairs that lead to Lord Bountiful's secret tower. You've never been here and all of a sudden you feel a little queasy. You hesitate.

Up, grunts the girl. Her arms are crossed like a mud wrestler's. She's not a girl to take her duty lightly.

You snort at her in a superior fashion, then gather the skirts of your party dress, taking care to conceal your lump, and slowly start to climb the stairs. The dark grey walls are lit every few feet by flickering candles. The higher you get, the fewer candles there are. The corridor is dark and cold. It's damp as you approach the landing, and so dark you can't see the door. You stop on the landing.

You're supposed to knock, says the girl.

You bite your lower lip.

You know how to knock, she says, Knock.

You lift your dainty, manicured hand and fold it into a flimsy, incompetent fist. You tap your knuckles very gingerly.

There is a knocking at the door.

You're surprised when he responds so quickly. You can't believe he's even heard your wimpy tap, but he roars, Come in! He's been waiting for you.

When you hear his voice you gulp. You look at the coffee girl and smile, suddenly friendly. She's turning away.

Hey, you whisper to her, Where you going?

Back to work, she says outloud.

You shush her, then catch yourself and smile like you and she are old buddies. Hey pal, you whisper conspiratorially, help out a friend in need, will ya? Get me outta here? You clutch at the lump that's loosening in your skirts.

The girl smiles at you like she's known you for a long, long time, reaches behind you, turns the handle of the door and pushes you in.

Don't leave me, you whisper to her. But she's closed the door behind you.

The walls of the vast dark panelled room are covered with hunting trophies. You see the heads of deers and boars and hogs and pigs and rats. And at the far end of the room, above the desk he's sitting at, is a head you can't see clearly enough to identify the species. He sits behind his wide oak desk and smokes a fat cigar. You press yourself against the door.

Somebody didn't come, he grunts, no longer the suave, distinguished gentleman who took you in his arms so long ago.

Pardon me? You use your meekest who-me voice. You flutter your eyelashes, forgetting for a moment he's too far away to see.

You sent an invitation to somebody who didn't come, he says. Who didn't you tell me about?

For once, you're speechless. You shrug, hoping the shoulder of your wonderful dress will slip enough to show your smooth white skin and coax him to forget his anger. But Lord B is not moved.

It wasn't me, you say with your righteous voice. It must have been that awful flashlight girl, stealing an invitation to send to one of her hoodlum chums.

He crosses his arms. The flashlight girl loathes these kinds of do's. She's in the kitchen playing poker with her pals.

Well, I must have forgotten, you lie, But I have the guest list in my room. I'll go have a look at it and let you know. You smile as innocently as you can.

Lord Bountiful slaps the armrests of his chair. He's about to shout, but he clears his throat instead. He straightens his tie and sits back in his chair. Fine, he says, Perhaps you'd like to run to your room and bring the list back to me?

Why, sure, you stutter, not quite believing he's letting you out of his sight so easily.

Behind you the door is opening by itself.

I'll be back in a jiffy, you chirp and slip out of the room.

When the door creaks closed behind you, he rubs his hands.

You don't go to your room, of course. You know that whatever you tell him about your secret guest, he'll finish you. You can't go back to him. But you also know that wherever you go in his house, they'll have their eyes on you. As they also will in his city. He owns the world. There's no place you can go where he hasn't posted his guards. There's no place you can get away.

Well, maybe one. A place so low and grimy and gross and poor the guards don't like to get their boots messed up by going there. It's the place you belong, Lady Bountiful.

You're coming back to me.

You stumble down the steps. You're tripping over your disgustingly costly ballgown. You're trying to calculate how long he'll give you in your room before he comes to look for you. You wonder how far you can get before he and his guards mount up and gallop after you. You limp through the galleries of the private quarters. Your burden seems heavier as you run. It rubs against your skin beneath your skirt. You don't stop at your room, you tumble down the stairs. You hobble past the library and the billiard room and card rooms. You go down the skinny ladder to the bowels of the building – the beery, steamy, sweaty smelling kitchen. The shelves of which are piled high with bones of chicken and duck and cow and sloppy, finger-licked bowls of avocado and onion dip. On the floor are tubs of melting ice and empty booze and bubbly bottles. There's plastic garbage bags full of empty cans and a couple of overindulged coffee-cart girls trying to sleep the party off. The flashlight girl and half a dozen of her pals are ignoring the mess and ignoring the jobs they ought to be doing. They're sitting around a card and bottle and ashtray covered table playing poker. You cluck and start to scold the disobedient girls, but you remember why you're here.

You hobble to the flashlight girl. Let's go, you order, I'm leaving.

The flashlight girl ignores you. Gimme two, Lulu, she says to the dealer. Lulu is wearing a – stolen! – pillbox hat. But you don't notice this.

Pardon me, you snort to the flashlight girl, I don't plan to go there on my own.

Say what? shouts Lulu. The ghetto blaster perched on top of the deepfreeze is pumping out The Greatest Hits of Marvin Gaye, Volume One and it is difficult to hear what people say.

Two, the flashlight girl repeats, and she thrusts up two fingers at you. Her pals laugh at her gesture. Lulu deals her a pair.

You shift your bag beneath your skirt and kneel down by her. I'll give you a million, you say, I'll make you rich – I'll never – Don't let me go alone, I'll never, I'll always —

The flashlight girl brushes you away. Her buddies laugh at the transparent promises you never keep.

It takes you a minute to register that you've actually been turned down. You push yourself off the floor, heave your burden up and make a beeline for the servants' ladder.

At the front door, you try to convince the cloakroom girl that one of the coats is yours. Your run through the house and your panic has dishevelled you. You look like a used-up slut. The cloakroom attendant eyes you skeptically, but then decides to enjoy the spectacle of your wriggling into the meagre polyester shawl she throws you. When you ask her to call you a cab, she laughs and jabs her thumb towards the door.

It's wet and cold and dark outside, and your tattered ballgown and your shredded dancing shoes, your ornamental shawl, can hardly begin to keep the cold away. You shiver and, like a little girl wearing high heels for the first time, fall down the steps to the cab waiting at the bottom.

The cabbie mistakes the way your mascara is smeared and the snuffly noises you make for those of a jilted call girl. He lets you hoist yourself into the cab and refuses to budge until you pay him in advance. You root around in the shawl and find, miraculously, in a concealed pocket, a twenty dollar bill. You thrust the crunched-up bill at him. He holds it to his flashlight to check it isn't fake, pockets it, clicks his tongue. The horses lurch.

Once the cab is clacking along, you pull the curtain aside and look back at the palace. Behind you, like a melting confectionery ornament, it shrinks. When you can no longer see it you drop the curtain. It's dark inside the cab, and for the first time in a long time, you're alone. You lean your head against the seat and sigh.

I wish that, given this perfect chance, this perfect setting and perfect time, you'd think. I wish, against the backdrop of the cold black sky, you would reflect upon what you have done and have a flash of insight or of clarity. Perhaps it isn't too late. Perhaps you could, perhaps... You don't, not yet, but I still hope you will someday. Someday I want you to know what you did. But it won't be today.

You put your fingers to your lips. You cock your head the way you always used to do, to help you decide the most useful thing to say. The words come naturally to you. You only have to rehearse them once. Then you loosen the bag beneath your skirt and place it on the seat beside you. You pat it so it's comfy then you lay your head on it – it's warm – and then you sleep.

The driver wakes you up.

Out! he yells.

You stick your head out the window. But we aren't there yet, you huff, I paid you twenty bucks.

I don't go no further than this, girlie.

I'm not a girlie, you snap, I'm Lady Bountiful.

The cabbie turns around to look at you. In the rain your makeup is running and your hair is dripping down in knots.

Right doll, the cabbie chuckles. Now be a good girl and get outta my cab.

You press your back to the seat and cross your ankles and fold your hands in your lap like a matron who will not be moved.

He leans down to open the door. *Get out.*

You sit still, staring in front of you. He grabs the front of your dress – you hear it rip – and hurls you into the street. You fall down on the wet hard stones. He flicks his whip and off the horses trot. From where you lie you see the horses' hooves with their heavy, metal shoes. The cab has left you outside the ghetto gate. You used to walk through this gate every day when you worked beneath the ground. Tonight, against the dirty wet sky, the gate looks thicker than you remember it. You don't think why this is. You pick yourself up and walk through the gate. You walk back to where you used to live with me.

You limp off balance from your skirt. And though it's dark and you can't see, you remember how to find me by the touch. I'm waiting for you. I'm sitting behind the door and I am listening. I hear you stumble against the garbage cans and slip on papers and I hear the dull whap of the bag beneath your clothes.

Through the crack in the door I see you. You're flushed and bruised and limping. You're crying. You lean your body against the door. You press your open palm against the door. You're trying to talk. I see your mouth move but you're so exhausted you can't speak. You lift your skirt. You cry as you untie, then remove, like a dismembering, the bag.

You lift it. You press it to the door. It covers the crack. I can't see you now. But your other hand is free.

There is a knocking at the door.

Though I don't ask you who you are, you say, It's me.

I don't say anything. For a minute you're quiet, then you knock again.

Behind you, past the alley, is a clacking sound.

I've brought something for you.

I don't say anything.

You have to raise your voice because the sound in the ghetto behind you is getting louder.

Here it is. You hit the bag against the door. It makes a wet, thwapping sound. When you remove the bag to hit the door, I see through the crack. You're crying hard. Your face is a mess of mascara, as blue as ink, as black as a mine. Your other hand isn't knocking anymore, it's scratching. Your hand is raw. The tips of your manicured fingernails are breaking.

Let me in.

You still expect me to be fooled by your sniffles and apologies.

You say, as if you're telling me something I don't know, as if you're having a revelation, They're after me.

I could have told you long ago that this would happen Someday. I could have told you how you'd hurry back and say what you are saying now to coax me. But I guess I didn't know all your tricks because what you say next – and for only the second time in our star-crapped lives – surprises me. So much I can't even open my mouth to speak. You open your mouth and whisper, you whisper so sweetly it almost could sound true, you say, you say, I didn't mean to leave you.

Immediately, as if even you can't believe what ludicrous syllables have sputtered from your blue-black mouth, you say again, I didn't mean to leave you.

What I don't mean is to let you leave again.

Behind you, up the alley, I see the eager, heaving bodies of the horses.

I open the door. You fall inside. I catch you and the bag. You try to close the door behind you as if that could stop them, but I don't let you. I keep the door wide open. I want them to find us like this. You try to stand, you try to leave, again, but this time I hold you so tight you can't. I slap the bag across your neck and drag you and it over me. I feel the awful, familiar heat, the messy wet of the bag, and I feel you, whining and struggling beneath it, and still, still making excuses. You're close to me, so close that when you stop chattering you hear, despite the noise of the stampede, what I've desired to tell you for so long: Look, look, you stupid bitch, here come the horses.

This is how you're trampled in my arm.

DR FRANKENSTEIN, I PRESUME

I AM IN MY bed and almost out, and almost where I can forget. But just when I'm about to fall, my loyal dark assistant is beside my bed. She shakes me awake. I see her masked face, pale as a moon. Her mouth moves underneath her mask. Doctor, she rasps, There's going to be a storm.

Then I'm in my boots, tucking my pj's into my overcoat. My eyes are half-shut. I stumble through the dark, suddenly cramped and twisting hall of my condo. The walls start to melt like silly putty in fire. My neat framed prints of Erte and O'Keefe begin to shake. I fumble with the buttons on my coat. My loyal dark assistant tosses me my bag. We stumble out to a waiting cab. I hear the hum of the fuel-injected engine, the steel radials on the smooth asphalt. But between the shifts of gears, I hear the neigh of horses, the clack of hooves on cobblestones. Beside me in the creaking cab, I see flashes of orange fluorescent lights, then the green of gas lamps playing on my dark assistant's face.

We rush through red lights without stopping. At this late hour there's no one on the country roads that wind up to where we're going. The buggy stops. I tumble to the castle in the rain. The giant wooden door creaks open in front of me. I push through the heavy beige doors of the emergency room. They swing behind me like that opening scene in the Dr. Kildare reruns. I run down the shiny hospital-green corridor. Bats fly in the tall gothic arches above us. I hear the crack of lightning, the roll of thundrous, though not entirely convincing, kettle drums, the hum of incandescent lights, my panting breath. I hear my loyal dark assistant's rubber soles squeaking behind me.

I throw off my coat and drop my pj's on the floor. I want to fold them neatly so they won't remind me of when I tore my clothes off in desire. But my loyal dark assistant hurries me, Doctor, Doctor, it's time.

My assistant helps me don my spotless-as-a-bride white gown. I scrub up until I'm pink and raw, my skin so soft it throbs. I slip my fingers in the tight, constricted gloves. My covered hands look ghostly, smooth. My head feels pinched in my doctor's cap when my assistant pulls my hair back. I look like a nun. The mask is soft when it brushes my skin. My dark assistant ties me in.

I walk towards the operating room, my hands held high, my white starched sleeves rolled up. My elbows press against the swinging doors. Inside, the ceiling, floor and walls are blindingly white. White light shoots down from a giant lamp. I hear the crack of lightning and look up. Thirty feet above us a skylight stretches towards the stormy sky.

My loyal dark assistant, a Jackie Coogan hump pressing up through the back of her polyester nurse's blouse, shuffles around a huge, monstrous bed. Leather straps hang off the shaky frame of metal 2 x 4's that support the bed. Despite myself, I hear a very Vincent Price sounding chuckle rise up in my throat. On rickety tables around the bed, jars of gory red, unearthly green are stewing. My eyes leap like a close-up camera to an opaque fuchsia fluid pumping up and down a tightly twisted coil. Something viscous bubbles in a big black cauldron. My eyes snap to green lines blipping on a screen, the erratic landscape of vital signs. I look out the stone-framed, gothic window openings. Sharp mountain peaks are illuminated by furious bolts of lightning. Back on the vital sign screen, the green line dips abruptly into a valley then evens out to a very lifeless looking plain. Cut to a bright chrome tray of neatly laid out stainless steel knives and scalpels, cotton swabs and gauze. Conspicuously, in the middle of a tray, a mammoth, wooden-handled rusty knife twitches. A sharp chord jolts from an organ.

Cut to water dripping down dark grey stones upon which teeter my various diplomas from UCLA and Transylvania State. Cut to sweat popping on my brow, my tense, dramatic eyes, my trembling, entrusted-with-the-power-of-God hands, blue veins throbbing. Cut to my loyal dark assistant's back, now straight again beneath her polyester blouse, and the loose, seductive knot that keeps her tunic tied. Cut to me blinking. Cut to Igor-Coogan's hump bulging out of his ratty jacket. Cut to me shaking my head. Blinking. Her back flat again. Me blinking again.

Thunder crashes over the manic music of the organ. My eyes pop open. Cut to the glowing skylight above. Cut to bright silver lamp hanging from beige modern ceiling. Roll into it. Fuzz focus to white. Fade into crisp white sheet. Pull back to show the white sheet on the rickety bed raised toward the skylight. Close-up of thick, cracked leather straps with huge metal buckles. Pan the sheet beneath whose contours lie —

Did I forget to mention whose the body was? How could I? When there was only one, and only ever has been one, on whom I would be qualified to operate.

Perhaps I should have told you this before. But then, perhaps it's you who never should have told me what you did, repeatedly, again, again, and only when you knew I would say yes.

For I remember this: Your white back arcing in the dark. Your dark mouth open like a pool. The pact you said your body meant. The true and desperate way that I believed you.

I run my trembling eyes across the white pillow case, the one with the pretty yellow and white embroidered daisies. The scent of the sheets is sandalwood. The touch of the sheets is soft. The shape beneath the snow-white sheet, on this, the longest and the sweetest night in years, is you.

Lightning crashes. The screens that watch the vital signs go blip.

I step towards the raised-up bed. My rubber soles squeak. The lights are harsh. I blink. Spots of red pop in my eyes. I watch the sheet you lie beneath. I blink again.

A movement? Slight? Your teasing breath?

I remember your pulse, your words, dear love, your white back arcing in the dark.

My loyal dark assistant pulls the white sheet back so I can see your skin. I thrust my palm out to my dark assistant. She slaps a scalpel down. The metal is cool against my plastic glove. I trace the path above your skin where I will enter you.

I remember the skin of the cup of your throat, the quickening of your pulse. I remember the way your chest, then neck, then face got rose with color. I remember your white back arcing in the dark.

Lightning cracks. Machines go blip. I hold the scalpel poised.

I blink. I think I see a pulse. Your neck? But I am here to do a quickening, a bringing back from death. Unless I'm mistaken —

One white-gloved hand of mine presses your skin. The other draws a line above your chest. My first surprise – imagine my surprise! – it only takes a tiny tap to break. It's like I'm cutting into a quiche. I cut along a line expecting a sudden burst of red. But no, the knife comes clean, like a perfectly cooked cheese and mushroom quiche, not too dry, not too runny.

You aren't a bloody mess inside, the way you ought to be, the way every person I've ever had, or ever heard or read about has been. No, you really are like those naive textbook sketches they tried to teach me from in med school. Every nerve and tendon neat, each vein in line, each artery, the layers of your flesh pristine. You're pretty as a picture.

I touch the cutaway carefully. There is no blood. I squeeze the severed parts of you the way I'd squeeze open the two halves of a baked potato, and stick my hand inside your chest.

I stretch my fingers in until I feel something, a hard thing. I pull the skin away from it. I squint.

Nurse, I rasp. I recognize it.

A heart. Sort of. A tough pink little valentine of sugar, color, corn starch. A candy heart. I wipe my trembling hand across it and read your words: *You're mine.*

Nurse, I groan. She daubs my brow. I squint, looking deeper in your chest to see the color of the candy heart is changing: sky blue. The red letters change too: *Kiss Me.*

Nurse, I moan, Nurse?

I try to hold your heart in my hands, but I can't keep it from changing. Your heart is green. It says, *Hot Stuff.* Then – pink, white, yellow – like the horse of a different color in *The Wizard of Oz.* Your heart is a rainbow of sweet, after-dinner mint pastels, each printed with some cute little words.

Scalpel, I growl to my dark assistant, but she's already pressed the sharp edge to my palm. I poke your heart. I expect it to crumble into sticky, powdered sugar. When the knife makes contact, it scrapes but doesn't give. Though I pull at it, the surrounding tissue doesn't move. When I pull the flesh away, I see this heart is not connected to a thing. Your artificial heart has natural bypass. It still says words. It tells me *Trust me. Kiss Me. You Belong to Me. You're Mine. Kiss me.*

My stomach clenches. I try to look away from you but I can't.

Was it my fault I didn't accurately diagnose the symptoms?

Symptoms? What symptoms? There hadn't been any goddamned symptoms. I had nursed you and given you more than the ounce of prevention anyone – even you – deserved. And even if there had been symptoms, I wouldn't have been able to diagnose them. Because you were something they didn't teach about in med school, a whole new life – or something – support system. You weren't what you appeared to be, what you had said you were to me.

You'd said it to me as trusting and innocent-seeming as anyone, the first time you had come to me. I'd asked you to answer a few brief questions from our medical history form regarding your record of illnesses, hospitalizations, allergies, diet, susceptibilities, proclivities, tendencies, desires. I'd asked you all of that in good faith, and listened to you, and checked off the appropriate boxes in good faith. And what you told me was a load of crap.

I now see that you go against the given on which the entire history of western medicine, not to mention everything you ever said to me, has been based.

But supposing, just supposing, that you had told me the truth when you'd first come to me. Would I have believed you? When what that awful truth was, was beyond belief? When what you would have said, if you had ever said the truth, was that the most you've ever been is less than human, a bloodless, heartless, pretty-faced cadaver?

How did you do it, darling?

Nurse! I croak, my jaw trembling, my eyes about to let loose a flood of tears. But I stop myself. I sniff, then thrust my firm young jaw against the wind, which has suddenly begun to howl through the interior of the lab. Nurse! I snap efficiently. I'm going to be big about this. I am going, despite the anguish it will cause me, to observe this for a greater cause, for science, for the rest of humanity, the poor bastards.

Nurse! I yell.

I hear the swish of my dark assistant's lab coat, then the squeak of her shoes, the clanging of a door. I drop my noble pose and turn around to see my dark assistant has abandoned me. She's left me here alone.

With you.

I look down at your perfect skin, the dark line where the scented sheet touches you. I look down at your candy heart, its words and colors changing.

I hear blood beating in my brain. I hear —

You sigh. Your eyes slide open sleepily. As if you've only been asleep. You open your pretty brown eyes that sweet, slow way you always used to when you were about to have me. You look so sweet and sleepy I almost raise my fingers to your cheek the way I used to. Until I remember, almost with surprise, that both my hands are clenched inside your body.

Our eyes meet. Then, sleepily, you close yours.

I watch your peaceful face and I dig my fingers into your candy heart. The muscles in my arms and hands pull taut. I squeeze harder, trying to strangle.

You don't flinch.

I lean over your pretty face and ask you, Don't you feel this?

My heart beats, waiting for your voice.

You sound sweet and syrupy. Feel what?

This. I press my fingers harder inside you.

What? You pout because I've interrupted your nap.

Don't you feel this? I mash my hands together hard.

There is a pause.

What? You're petulant. I don't feel a thing.

Keep your eyes closed, I say. Tell me when you feel something.

I clench my hands around your slippery heart. I take a deep breath. Then I rip it out of you.

Your white back doesn't arc.

I hold your heart above your pretty body. Your eyes stay closed.

Do you feel that?

You shake your sleepy head.

I carry your heart across the room. It weighs almost nothing. I stretch my white sleeves towards the light above me. I watch the changing colors and the silly changing words: *You're Mine. I'm Yours. I Love You. Kiss me.*

Then I hear you speaking words out loud.

When are you going to do it? I'm tired of lying here.

I look back at you, comfy on the bed. You have no idea what has been ripped out of you. Suddenly, your heart is heavy on my arms. I want to lower it, to dump it back inside you, but my arms lock. I buckle, about to fall, but my legs are stiff. I teeter but I can't fall.

When are you going to do it? you whine.

I open my mouth to answer you, but I can't speak. I want to look away from you, so calm and pretty on the bed, but my head is locked. My arms tremble under the weight. I want to drop it but I can't let go.

WHAT I DID

My job was to carry the bag. I carried the bag by the rope. The rope had been run through the reinforced holes in the top of the bag. The top of the bag was gathered neatly and firmly by the rope and the rope was knotted and kept the bag closed. A couple of feet of the end of the rope was what I held to carry the bag. I hoisted the bag up and bore it on my back. I bent beneath the weight of it. The bag was heavy. The bag was about 2½ feet long, full, though not entirely full, there was some give in the bag, some looseness, but nonetheless so heavy I could not, I am sure, have carried the bag if the bag had been entirely full. The material of the bag was leather or some similarly sturdy fabric. The bag appeared to be impermeable. That is, I never saw leaking from the bag. Though in truth, what I saw was not a lot. It was hard to see. But I had felt the bag carefully and had never felt anything that felt like a seam, nor pattern of weave nor pores. I speculated there were none. In fact, to be honest, what I said about the reinforced holes at the top of the bag, was only speculation. I hadn't seen the reinforced holes, though I had looked as closely and carefully as I could, but it was always, even when it was not entirely, dark.

There was a thing inside the bag. Which though solid shifted sometimes when I picked the bag up or set it down or stumbled under it. I carried it on my back. The rope was over my shoulder, my hand holding the end of it tightly, the bag on my back. Sometimes I held my fist around the rope right in front of my chest. Bearing the bag on my back, I bent beneath it. Sometimes I felt the contents of the bag, which was one thing, though of two parts, shift. Sometimes nearer my shoulders, sometimes nearer the small of my back, sometimes to either side of me. I knew it was not more than one thing, though it was in two parts, because sometimes when it shifted, one part fell to my left, the other to my right, but it was always connected, there was no break between these parts. And sometimes part of it moved although the other part was still. But there was never a separation; inside the bag was one, not two. It was this thing inside the bag it was my job to carry.

When the bag was to be moved, I was summoned by the light. There was no light except the light. And the light only shone when I should move the bag. All otherwise was dark.

The light summoned me. I scrambled up from my place of rest and fumbled across the yard to the spotlit path at the edge of the yard where the bag sat in the spot of light. I squatted down. I took the rope in my hand and I turned on the balls of my feet so the bag was behind me. I gripped the rope tightly and pulled the bag up on my back. I felt the bag lift off the ground and hit the small of my back just above my shorts. The rope rubbed my shoulder and my collar bone through my t-shirt and I felt the skin of the bag on the skin of my back through my shirt. I stood up stumbling. I got my balance. The bag was very heavy and with my head bent down and my stomach squished and neck twisted, my sense of balance was not all it should have been. I didn't have much time to right myself because the light was moving away. I heaved myself up and carried the bag where the light led me down.

The spot of light on the path reminded me of the bouncing ball in old movies when you're supposed to sing along by following the ball bouncing along over the words of the song and you have to keep up or you'll be left behind.

The sound of the light was a hum, as efficient and sometimes as irritating as a refrigerator. Like a refrigerator it sometimes clicked off. Those were the times I wasn't carrying, and everything was dark.

What I saw of the path was what the light illuminated, a small black, though rendered grey, like slate beneath the light, dry and cracked and split-up bit of ground. And walls. The path was straight, as straight as if a beam of light had bored down into it, more smooth than any blast, and narrow, a few inches wider than an outstretched arm. Not that I could ever outstretch my arm. Not while I carried the bag.

I walked down the path exactly as I was led which prevented me from knocking into the wall on either side of me, which prevented me from putting extra pressure on my hand and on my always aching back and shoulder. The skin of my shoulder was tender. As soft as pimento as cool as a spoon. I had never formed a callus. Walking down the middle of the path also prevented me from stepping too near the walls which I was not permitted to do. But sometimes, I stumbled and fell against a wall. Because of the dimness I couldn't see and because of my hand around the rope I couldn't touch, but I heard the thwap of the bag and the crumbling of chunks breaking off the walls. But other times when I fell to the side I didn't hear anything except the whup of me dropping the bag and the thud of me on the ground. But I didn't hear any crumbling because I hadn't bumped into a wall because some places off the path weren't walls but openings.

Whereinto the light led not.

I carried the bag where I was led. When the light stopped, I stopped. I did not step beyond the light. I dropped the bag. The bag hit the ground with a thud. What was in the bag shifted. I sank down with weariness. But I couldn't sit there and rest, the light wouldn't wait for me. It started going back up the path back to the yard. I stumbled up and followed the light back up.

The return trip was up the same path and between the same walls. In a way it was as hard as the downward trip because though I wasn't carrying the bag, I was going up. The path was a very steep incline. Very often on this trip I thought I was about to fall – no, really, truly about to tumble back and fall back down. I was afraid to fall, I didn't want to fall down there and I could imagine rolling down, I didn't know where I could stop. But on the other hand, though I had no other hand, I would have been relieved to stop carrying the bag. But always just before I fell I would suddenly be able to make out, as if by some sudden brightness of the light, the yard.

When I got back to the edge of the yard, to the spot where I'd collected the bag, the light went out. It was perfectly dark again and perfectly quiet. Besides myself the only sound was the moving light. It hummed. When it went out, there was only me.

I shuffled my way in the dark to my resting place in the yard. Finding my way even this short distance was difficult. I couldn't see. I walked along so slow and stiff, my arm swinging in front of me like a trunk or a tentacle to try to feel what I couldn't see. I slipped my feet along, feeling for my resting place. Or sometimes I crawled along on my knees, my hand along the ground looking for the dip. When I reached my resting place I felt around for my cup. My cup was full when I came back and I drank from it. But sometimes I misjudged where I was or I was so thirsty and eager or tired and I kicked it over and spilt it and it was sucked into the ground. The ground was dry and I could hear the water sinking in, it made a hissing sound. When that happened I got nothing and I was thirsty and I had to wait until the next time I came back after carrying the bag.

My place of rest was a slight depression, not quite a hole in the ground, almost as deep as me. But part of me, no matter how flat I lay, remained above the level of the ground. I had made the depression to lie in by digging up the ground. The ground was hard but I worked it hard and made a hole to contain me. I could almost lie flat on my back, side or stomach, using my hand under my head as a pillow. Or if I hoped to minimize the brightness or the light when it would summon me, I would put my hand over my eyes to shield the light or lie as flat, as far down as I could so the light might reach me less. But every time when I woke, I'd shifted in my sleep, my body had moved, and I lay exactly where the light speared in to summon me.

When the light summoned me by shining in my eyes, I scrambled up and trudged across the yard to the spotlit bag. I picked up the bag and, bent beneath the bag, I followed the light down. When the light stopped, I stopped. I dropped the bag and sank with weariness.

Sometimes after I dropped the bag, I wondered. What if I just waited until I'd really caught my breath the way I needed to, would the light wait for me? But every time I tried to wait, it didn't wait, and I couldn't resist. It started back up without me and the fear that it would not come back and that I'd be left down there in the dark made me go with the light.

My job was to carry the bag and I did my work hard. I was conscientious. I didn't cheat. I didn't cut corners. I didn't go on strike. I didn't complain. Well, not much. Rather, not out loud. My voice in the silence and the dark sounded too alone. And who would have heard? But I did wonder.

I wondered how the bag got from the bottom of the path where I left it to the spotlit place by the yard where I picked it up. Sometimes when I lay in my resting place I listened, but I never heard the sound of anything except the hum of the light and me. But always when I woke the bag had been transported up the path by some great mystery.

This time when I was summoned, I was eager. I hurried to the spotlit bag and hoisted it and hauled it down. When the light stopped at the bottom of the path, I stopped. I dropped the bag. But when the light bounced up the path again, I didn't follow it. I stayed where I was. I caught my breath. When the light had gone, I was left in the dark. I held the rope. I felt the roughness of the rope in my palm. I turned on the balls of my feet so the bag was behind me and I gripped the rope and pulled the bag up on my back. I took a couple steps and stumbled. It was hard going up with the bag on my back. I couldn't imagine how anyone could. But I righted myself and took a few more steps before I stumbled again. I stumbled to my left and knocked against a wall. Chunks crumbled. I righted myself, stumbled a few paces more then swerved to my right. My body knocked against a wall. I tottered up then stumbled another couple of paces and this time I fell against nothing: I was beside an opening. I went into the opening. I hauled the bag with me and went into the alley. When I got as far as I thought was necessary – further than the spillover of the light of the path could reach – I dropped the bag. I sat down. I leaned my back against the wall of the alley and caught my breath. The bag lay at my feet like a loyal dog. I touched the bag, running my hand over it. Its skin felt slippery where it had hit the walls. The walls were wet. I kept my hand on the bag a minute, then patted the bag. I stood up and turned around and walked off. I left the bag.

I wasn't used to walking without the weight of the bag and bowed beneath it, so I wandered. I bumped into what I hadn't on the way into the alley – big corrugated metal trash cans, clumps of soggy paper, broken glass and piles of things that clattered. It was a dreadful place where I'd not been allowed to come. I left the alley running.

I knew I'd reached the path when I fell sideways down an incline. I picked myself up and climbed as fast as I was able to the yard.

When I got to my resting place I was very thirsty. I reached out for the cup but knocked it over. I heard the water spill and make a hissing sound as it sank into the ground. I didn't put the cup down. I held it and held it in my hand as if by some good mystery it would be full again.

I lay down in my resting place and looked forward to a long, uninterrupted and true rest. I wouldn't have to carry the bag again.

But this time when I rested, how I dreamt of my bag! Now since I had tried to hide it, I thought of it as "mine." I dreamt that I was walking and I didn't have the weight on me and I was on a different path. I was walking somewhere open, I'd been walking long and it was light, not just the light, but light like daylight, with nothing between me and the sun but sky. Then there was a hand, and then the hand was pointing and I saw the bag. I kneeled on the moist ground in the open air beneath the blue, blue sky and slowly, slowly put my hand around the bag. The bag was warm. The bag was soft as skin. I could feel through the thinness of the bag to the thing inside, and I knew what it was. Then easily, so easily, the bag opened itself to me, the rope coiled at the top of the bag unwound, the skin slipped apart like oil, it opened like a bud and there was a sweet, clean smell like a blessed thing, like a thing released. I looked down in the bag and saw —

The light. The light was waking me. I closed my eyes and tried to will myself to sleep again because though in the dream I knew what was in the bag before I opened it, I didn't know awake. But I couldn't sleep.

Across the yard in the spotlit spot was the bag. It had been found and moved from where I'd hidden it. I pulled myself up from my resting place. My hand still held the cup which I'd hoped would, by some good mystery while I still slept, be filled. I slipped the cup into my shirt. The metal was cool against my skin. I walked to the spotlit place and took the rope and heaved the closed bag up on my back and followed the light down the path.

When the light stopped at the bottom of the path, I stopped too. Though I dropped the bag, I continued to hold the rope. I sank down as always but this time when the light started to bounce back up the path, I stayed. I sat on the ground. I watched the path until it was no longer lit by the departing light. Everything was dark. I blinked as everything got black and I could not see. I pulled my bag more close to me. I felt the bag next to my ribs. I stuck my hand in the air like a trunk or a tentacle and I felt nothing. The ground beneath was crumbly with patches of oiliness or wet. The only sound was my breath. The light was gone, I couldn't hear its hum.

I put my hand around the bag. I felt with my fingertips and palm the texture of the outside of the bag. It was like leather or some similarly sturdy, flexible fabric. I found no seams, nor pores nor weave. Though the bag was full, it was not entirely full. There was some give and looseness. I was able to move the surface of the bag over different parts of the thing inside without moving the thing inside itself. I couldn't tell if the bag was warm, or had been made so from its having been held next to me. Also what was in the bag, though solid, gave slightly to the pressure of my hand. There was the ssshhh sound of my hand moving along the bag. Then there was the sound of the flap of the cloth as my hand went in my shirt and brought the tin cup out. I knocked the cup against the ground. Bits crumbled. My hand got gritty. I kept hitting the cup against the ground until it bent. I broke it where it bent to make a scalpel or knife.

I stuck the point of the knife into the middle of the knot and tried to pull the knot apart; it wouldn't budge. I tried with my hand and teeth and with the knife to undo the knot but it was fast. I tried to cut the rope. I sawed at the rope but the strands wouldn't cut. What cut was the insides of my fingers that held the knife. My hand stung with sweat and the wet knife slipped.

I lay the bag on the ground. I pressed the contents of the bag as flat as it would go. I ran my hand over the surface of the bag to find the place that gave most easily. I drew a line in the air above that place where I would enter in. I thought it would only take one tiny scalpel tap to split the surface of the bag. It didn't. I pressed and gouged and poked and hacked but the skin of the bag was tough. It didn't sever. Not like me, not like my skin. As I hit and hit and hit the bag my knife cut into my palm and fingers deeply. I felt the bag get wet from me, and I was glad I could see nothing in the dark.

I gave up. I wiped the knife against the ground and then against my shorts to wipe the excess off. I put the knife back in my shirt. I felt around to get my bearings where the path went up. I took the end of the rope in my hand and stood up. I dragged the bag back up the path. I shuffled slowly. It felt so different to drag the bag, to hear it scraping on the ground and not have its weight on my back. In the darkness my feet found the way. They felt the small dip in the middle of the road which had been pressed down by my treading. I could smell the wet smell of the walls I'd never paid attention to before. I could feel how cool and close were the narrow walls and I heard the ground beneath my feet.

Suddenly I was covered with affection for these familiar things. They had been true and stayed with me; they had been part of my job. My job had been but to carry the bag. Not to know why, nor how it kept coming back. My job was not to know its terrible contents.

I also knew that having once – no, twice – not done my job I could no more do it again. And I was tired. When I'd dragged the bag back to the edge of the yard where always before I'd found it, I didn't leave it. I dragged the bag across the yard. I dragged it to my resting place. I dropped the rope. I kneeled down. I took the bit of broken metal from inside my shirt and started digging. The ground was hard and dry but it broke easily. It opened as if to welcome me. Every handful was a gift, it was the good ground giving way to me. I picked the chunks of true ground out. I scooped the small bits and the dust. I made the hole the ground gave up more deep than where I rested. I made the hole about two feet long, and then a bit, and not as wide around. It was more like a shaft than a dip in the ground. When I dug how far the hole should be, the ground was getting moist. It felt less of the crust and more the heart of earth. I picked the bag up by the rope. I stood up. I lifted my arm and lowered the bag. When I felt the bag reach the bottom of the hole I was glad. I kneeled by the hole and coiled the rope on the top of the bag. I kneeled by the hole in the ground and imagined I could see down into it. I imagined the way it might look on a day with sun. I imagined I saw the bag at rest, the rope coiled in a circle on the top and the black and crumbling wall of earth around it. I closed my eyes though it made no difference in the dark, and kept them closed some moments. I wanted to say good words but I didn't know them.

I knew that it was good and right and meet and just, and in true time, this burying. But part of me was sad to inter the body of the bag.

I opened my eyes and threw a handful of dirt on the bag. The earth made a sound when it fell on the bag, I let there be quiet for a moment, then I threw the other dirt in. When the bag was covered and the hole was filled, I patted the dirt. I made the ground smooth over the bag. I couldn't see how visible it might be, where I had laid the bag, but I ran my palm across the ground to make it very smooth, to leave no sign of what I did.

Because of the bag, not all the dirt would fit back in that place. I pushed the dirt beside my resting place. I lay down in my resting place and closed my eyes. I reached my arm up from where I lay and swept the dirt from the hole for the bag onto me. I felt the sprinkles of the earth on me, as gentle as kisses but kisses that stayed, then covered me like a blanket and kept me down and held me down, not hard, not how I didn't want, but how I wanted. I swept it all so the ground by me was smooth. I tucked my arm beside me in the dirt. There wasn't enough to cover me entirely, but I did what I could.

I lay in my place of rest and listened. I heard my breath and when I breathed I felt the earth above me rise and fall. Besides my breath I heard one thing: the sound of something near me, in the earth. Like the slow small sound of a small thing when it's closing.

And when I heard, I pictured in my mind the bag beneath the ground. I saw the brown-grass color of the rope get black and wet, and saw its firmness relax, and I pictured the slow and good dissolving of the rope, the turning of the rope to ground. I saw the skin of the bag get thin as it did not resist the slow decay to earth. I saw flakes of the skin dissolve in patches. And then I saw the ground above break open and the light of open air, and then a hand pull back the earth and brush away the last flakes of the bag, and then that hand around the thing, exposed, that had been carried in the bag.

I saw this in my place of rest where I lay covered, waiting.

THE RUINED CITY

SHE SAID SHE WOULD go with me to the city.

I said, No.

You have to go.

I can't.

You left something there.

I shook my head.

She folded her arms and looked at me. She knew how to wait and how not to.

Who knows what's there, I mumbled. There could be gangs or dust or drought or poison air. I tried to tell her why without confessing.

OK, she said when I'd exhausted my excuses, What's the worst that could happen if you go back?

The worst? Oh, everything would be awful, but the worst, the *worst* – (I didn't want to say the worst) – I could die. I would, I would really die. We could both die if we went there, we would, we'd —

She'd never liked my flair for the dramatic.

One, she said, That's not the worst. Two, we probably wouldn't die. Three, you can't and I refuse to anymore, live without what you left in the city.

What I can't do is survive that trip. You know what I can't carry.

She didn't look away from me, my empty sleeve. She knew what I consisted of.

You can, she said, I'm going.

I wondered how I could stall for time. Should I tell her Someday? Wait?

It'll have to wait until the weather's better.

The weather is always the same.

It'll have to wait until the roads and until —

Not Someday. Now.

She started packing. She only packed essentials – food, water, knife, tarp, light. It all fit in her single bag.

And though I told her she should, she packed neither a passport nor a weapon.

How will you find it?

The maps were gone. The roads that I remembered had been bombed, the bridges burnt.

I will.

You've never been there, you don't know where it is.

I'd never told her where I'd left. But even what I could have told would not have been enough. I had worked hard to not remember.

How will you get there?

I'll walk.

She put her arms through the straps of the pack and hoisted it up on her back. As she tied the belt of the pack around her waist she said, There's enough in here for both of us. Come with me.

She stepped outside.

I didn't want to stay where she had left. I walked through the door behind her.

I'd never told her where I'd left but she had looked and she'd uncovered evidence: burnt-edged letters, yellowed pages, ragged strips of documents that hadn't quite been shredded. Junk mail that meant more than it seemed. A trail of drops and bandages. A shovel and a cup. She'd learned as much about the city I had left as I – but different things. Though she didn't know the history, she had the insight of a foreigner. She saw as quaint what I'd thought monumental, of consequence what I'd dismissed, redeemable what I thought lost. She did not fear nor envy what I did.

She made me travel faster than I thought my body could. At first I could barely keep up with her. Sometimes when I thought I was going to fall, no, really, truly about to fall down, she'd stop. And then I'd sink and she would slip the bag off her shoulders and take out the blanket and make a pillow for me. She'd touch my forehead to make sure I was all right and I would close my eyes and rest.

But once I heard her rustling and opened my eyes to watch her kneeling on the ground not far from me, her open palms an inch above the earth. She turned her head to listen and then, as if she'd heard a cue, she lowered her hands flat. I saw the muscles of her back and neck and arms pull tight as she leaned forward to put her ear to the ground. As long as I kept watching her, she stayed there patient, waiting, as if she heard something beneath the ground.

She took us past the low, round hills to the far side of the country we'd grown used to. Outside the border where I'd felt safe, we were exposed to sun and heat and drought.

She rationed carefully and she was fair, but after a while we used up our provisions. When I lagged behind her, I saw the shape of the empty water bottle shifting back and forth in the bag.

We were walking on a high flat road.

This was a logging road, she said. She showed me where the evergreens had been. We walked through a checkerboard pattern of bald brown clearcut, slash-and-burn and saplings thin as barb wire. Behind us the mountain had been stripmined. A deep black wedge was exposed. The road was dry. I wanted a drink.

I saw a stream in the gully by the road.

Let's stop.

She kept walking.

I let her get a few paces in front of me before I squatted down and cupped my hand in the water and raised it to my lips –

Stop!

Startled by her voice, I spilt the water.

She yanked me away from the stream.

Look, she pointed to the dark grey corridor of shade above the stream. Sun shone through the yellow leaves and on the caramel-colored pebbles in the water. Way upstream, trapped behind a knot of twigs, I saw a puddle of rust-colored foam. When I raised my moist hand to my face it smelled sour. I shook it to get the water off. My hand stung. She dug up a handful of dirt and rubbed it against my hand until the dirt was dry then brushed it off. Red splotches were rising on my hand and wrist and forearm.

It's going to burn for a while, she said. You have to be careful.

I had to learn to live off the ruined land.

We walked a long time in a barren place. It was hot. We'd run out of water days ago. I kept looking, thinking I saw it, but when I blinked, the only thing in front of me was her. The shape of her body was wavy with heat. I squinted into blinding white. When I closed my eyes sand gritted my eyelids and I saw red. But I couldn't keep them open. Then when I closed them everything was black. I fell.

When I came to it was cool and dim. She was holding something wet against my forehead. When I looked up I saw stars.

Where are we?

Inside.

She squeezed some of the water from the cloth into my mouth. But those are stars. I tried to point.

Minerals, she said slowly. We're underground.

I tried to leave but she held me back.

There's water down here.

She handed me a cup.

Not only water —

Right. Not only water. There's this —

She clicked the flashlight up at what I'd thought were stars.

Up here is just the mouth, there's only flecks, but further in –

I know what's there, I snapped. Where's the way out?

She pointed to a door-sized opening behind me. When I turned to look, I could see the white dry desert outside.

She handed me the cup again.

In the open mouth of the cup, the water looked black. I couldn't see the bottom.

I knew how what was brought up from the ground was brought. I'd seen the earth gouged open, and the maimed and broken miners dropped down every day. I knew about the charred black bits of bodies buried underneath the ground.

What did you have to do to get that? I nodded at the cup.

All I had to do was walk. It's easy to get. You don't have to do anything terrible.

She nodded to the corridor in front of us.

It's not a mine. It wasn't blasted open. Drink that, she said, I'll show you.

I didn't know if I believed her, but I was thirsty. I took the cup and drank.

She tied a cord around the flashlight so it could hang around her neck. She tucked the backpack in the corner. She took my hand. Stay near me.

The corridor was only wide enough for one. I walked behind her, so close I heard the swish of her shorts and smelled her skin. From behind she was lit like a silhouette, the white of her flashlight surrounding her.

She led me down inside the earth.

The path was level, about as wide as an outstretched arm. But even though I was close to it, I couldn't see what it contained. Sometimes she ran her hand, with mine inside, along a part of the wall and let me feel, between the layers of crumbling earth, the hard smooth streaks like marble. Sometimes she stopped so abruptly I almost bumped into her, and cupped our hands over something round and cool.

Further in, the path got thin. The earth felt cool and damp. The air was still. The light around her skin condensed into a gold metallic border. When the corridor started descending and zigzagged back and forth, and when she felt me trying to pull away, she held me tighter. We're almost there.

The corridor dropped sharply, we were running, then suddenly we were splashed with cold. We were in a pool. The water stung when it found my cuts and scratches, but it was soft and slippery as I splashed it on my face. Nothing was floating on the surface. She waded in front of me, the black line inching up her thighs and the small of her back. The light she'd hung around her neck bobbed with her steps.

Hold this. She lifted the flashlight off her neck. As she stretched her elbow up, the light cast a huge shadow of her on the wall.

When I took the light she dipped her face and then her whole self in the water. I cast the light on the opening to the path where we'd come in, then slowly shone it around the shiny walls. The pool was small. I could see the water level on the wall rise and fall with her movements. In the wall opposite where we'd come in I saw another opening.

When she saw me wading towards it, she came with me. She climbed up the bowl-like curve of the pool then helped me up. We stood in a giant, high-domed room. I shone the light on milky walls and opalescent doors and pearly curtains. There were gold and white and coral-colored cones and solid icicles. I saw the shapes of a frozen horse and a silent bird and a cold, unblinking profile. I saw an arm, stiff, hard and white. I saw a fist arrested in a blow.

What is this, I whispered as if I was afraid I'd break a spell.

The ones that hang down are stalactites, and those – she pointed down by our feet – are stalagmites. Both of which are calcite deposits.

No, I pointed again. Don't you see —

I know you think they look like things you see above the ground, but these were here before those things. What you see above the ground are transient imitations of these constant things.

I looked at them and touched them with my hand and tried to shake them but they would not move.

They don't change, she said, Or only do so so slowly you couldn't notice the change unless you lived a couple thousand lifetimes. These caves were formed before we were, from heat inside the earth. Molten lava shifted and exploded. When the lava cooled it solidified into walls. Water condensed and cracked the solid rock to make the openings that led us here. The shapes you see are formed from water too. It drips through the roof of the cave and when it evaporates, it leaves a mineral deposit, and they build up to shapes that make you think of what you see above the ground.

I shook my head. It was hard to think so differently.

Listen.

We both held our breath. Everything was silent. Then from a far-off place we couldn't see, we heard, so quiet we almost missed it, the sound of a drop of water.

That's when I thought someday I might believe her.

She taught me how to read the land. And where to dig for roots and find pure water. She found the things we needed to survive in hidden places. Where I saw just a dusty gulch, she showed there'd run a river. Where I saw rutted barrenness, she showed where crops had fed a vital city. She picked up rough red rocks and told me, "Brick – a wall." Then "Glass – a window." "Hard earth – where the dead are laid."

Thus we approached the outlands of the city. The farms had stopped producing and the houses had fallen down. But some of these old homes had what we needed. When she decided to approach, we did so cautiously. We had to avoid setting off undetonated mines. Outside the door of the place she picked, she'd find me a spot of shade and make me rest while she went in to scavenge.

Before she went in any house she paused outside the door. She lowered her head and closed her eyes. After a few seconds she lifted her head and slowly, as if she was responding to an old and infirm host, pushed the door open and entered. Sometimes I heard her walking around inside these ruined houses, opening cupboards and slowly climbing stairs. She never kicked through things, but turned them over carefully. When she came out she brought a couple of unbent cans of food, a flashlight battery, a cup.

When I didn't need to rest as much, she brought me inside and taught me how to search for what we needed. I stood behind as she bowed her head and pushed open creaking doors. She tested the steps before she ascended, and ran her hands on banisters whose balconies had disappeared. I stared at curtains flapping over empty panes and furniture that had been overturned and smashed. We made gloves out of rags and masked ourselves to filter out the dust that we unsettled. She gave me the army knife she found and showed me how to coax open locks and untie what was bound. I wore the knife on a rope around my neck.

We poked through the wreckage with sticks and we moved stones aside, exposing in the ground beneath the near-decay of barely living things. I tried to look away but she insisted that only by searching the low, unlikely places could we find the goods we needed to survive.

When I got strong enough to scavenge on my own, we split up into separate routes. So while she sifted through the pantry, I rifled through the den's remains. I liked looking through things myself. Sometimes I didn't tell her what I found.

And then one time she came upon me thus.

We'd come to a broken down mansion. She'd gone to look in a basement and I'd climbed upstairs to a giant ballroom surrounded by unbelievably intact French windows. From the ceiling hung what was left of a chandelier. The sunlight through the windows threw odd flecks of light against the walls. The floor was a mess of broken tables and empty bottles and fallen plaster. As I walked through the room I kicked up dust. I was coughing, my eyes were stinging. In the rising dust I could almost see a crowd. I felt pressed in. I felt them moving around me. I needed air. I picked up a brick and heaved it through a window. Glass shattered. I threw another and another, and even after there was plenty of air, I kept throwing things. The gritty texture in my palm and the pull of the muscles in my arm and the zinging sound of the bricks in the air and the sharp crisp sound of the breaking glass made me feel great. I was leaning down for another brick when there was a voice behind me.

What are you doing?

I dropped the brick and spun around. She was so small in the great double doorway to the ballroom, and with her ragged clothes and tattered pack, she looked like a beggar girl.

What are you doing?

I – I scrambled for an excuse. Breaking windows.

Don't.

I wanted some air.

There's other ways of getting it. This place may have what we need to survive, but it isn't ours. You should watch what you help yourself to. Here —

She handed me a couple of cans of food she'd scavenged.

The part that's wrecked was wrecked by someone like you.

I wanted to deny that but I couldn't.

She looked around at the jagged glass.

Do what you want but I'm not going to stay and watch you.

She turned around and left.

I watched her leave from a window I had broken. Outside the house she looked back up to where I stood. I didn't wave down to her. She looked back at the way we'd come. She hesitated, then tightened the pack securely and continued walking towards the city.

I found her that night by the fire she'd built. I sat down just outside the circle of light made by the coals. From time to time one of the coals burst into flame. The sky looked thick like it was filled with dust. No stars were visible.

In the middle of the night I thought I heard her say something. I went to listen but she was still asleep. She'd kicked the blanket off. When I kneeled to tuck the blanket around her, I saw her as I'd never seen her before. Her hands and arms were scratched, her shoulders were bruised. Her face had wrinkles it hadn't when we'd set out. I saw it was hard for her to go to the city. I didn't know why she was doing it. I put her unresisting arms beneath the blanket.

I was covering last night's fireplace with dirt when she woke up. When she started to put the bag on her back, I said, I'll carry that.

She helped me put it on. She turned my body away from her. I felt her shift the weight to me. The pack was against my back but I felt the soft folds of the blanket inside it. The cord she tied around my middle had been rubbed smooth by her hands. The first few steps I stumbled, but I adjusted quickly to the weight. The bag fit me as if it had been made for me.

Both of us carried it after this; we traded it back and forth.

It was late when, far in front of us, we saw a house.

We can spend the night there, I said.

She didn't say anything.

As we got near the house I saw the roof was still intact. We won't even have to put up the tarp.

We will.

No, look, we've never seen a place so whole.

I know.

When we got to the fence of the house she stopped.

Aren't we going in?

She shook her head.

But we've been walking so long. I tried not to sound impatient. It'll be dark soon.

It was already getting dark.

Can I have the pack?

I slipped it off my back. She put it on the ground.

We'll need the flashlight inside.

No.

I didn't want to argue with her.

You go in.

Without you?

She nodded.

Why don't you rest in the house. I'm sure there's somewhere to sit.

No.

She lifted the latch of the gate. I stepped into the yard.

Long dry grass grew over the path. The windows of the house looked whole and most of the blinds were drawn. The swaybacked wooden steps creaked when I stepped onto the porch. The chain of the broken porch swing dangled like someone hung. I paused at the door the way she always did before she went inside a house. When I tried the door knob, it gave. I blinked. It was light inside. The furniture was upright and neat. There was an open landing upstairs and a hall. In the dining room in front of me the table was set. Before I took another step I was, like Goldilocks, imagining the clear pure well, the full-stocked pantry, comfy bed upstairs, the windows that could keep away the cold. I turned to go tell her we should stay here for a while, but when I did, I heard something from the living room. The door was ajar. I peered in and saw the grey-blue flicker of an old TV, and facing it, their backs to me, a couple of high-backed easy chairs. On the arm of one was a newspaper, and on the other I saw a hand.

I pushed the door open and went in the room. Over the top of the chair, I saw the back of a head. I heard breathing. I stepped in front of the chair.

It was you.

You were asleep. Your mouth was slightly open. Your breathing was not as sweet as it had been. Maybe it was the glasses having slipped down your nose that made you breathe like that. You didn't used to have them. But I think it was something else. Your face was fuller, you'd gained some weight and your skin was not as firm and tight and smooth as it had been. Your other hand was limp on the knitting in your lap, and your feet, in plain grey slippers, were perched on a footrest.

I sat on the edge of the footrest and looked at you. You were, despite how you had made me wait, and made me wait for nothing, and then, despite how I tried to forget and then to stay away from you, and despite the true and awful secret I had kept of you, still, still, to me most terribly, almost forgivably, beautiful. I sat on your footrest in front of you and as I watched you sleep, I was afraid you would, yes, you still could, open your pretty brown eyes and your lovely, sleepy, innocent-seeming mouth and tell me what I longed for you to say. Though I wanted you to, and knew you wouldn't, I still feared you would. And I didn't want now for you to persuade me to not go to the city.

The knife I wore around my neck swung back and forth between my shirt and my sweating skin.

I could have done it then, I could have, while you slept so pretty and so unaware in the living room, slipped the knife out of my shirt and hacked your heart right out of you.

Did I sense someone at the window, looking in? Waiting for me to come back out and go?

And did you sense me near you?

You must have. You opened your brown, brown eyes. You gasped. Hello.

You hesitated . . . Hello.

You turned to look at the living room door to make sure we weren't being seen. I looked outside; a shadow had passed the window.

What are you doing here?

I'm looking for something.

You put your hand over your mouth. Very quietly you said, There's nothing here.

I looked around your TV room and saw your favorite vase, but not your trophies, not your atlases. The wall above the mantel was empty. It seemed true what you said.

What did you do with it?

You took a deep breath. You faltered. Now you were careful with your words; I lost it.

You weren't lying now. I looked around again to see if I could see what made you different. The wall above the mantel was empty but on the mantel were some little ceramic figurines, peasant children and dogs and birds, like something you'd ordered from the back of a magazine. There was a sampler made from a kit on the wall. The hardbacks on the shelves were book club books. You lived in a quiet, ordinary house.

Why did you do it?

I don't know.

Then you said, like you were asking me for a kindness, you said, I'm sorry. You said it again, I'm sorry. You looked away from me. I'm sorry, I'm sorry it can't be undone. I'm sorry.

You didn't deny it anymore.

Please, you said, Please —

I heard in your voice how afraid you were. You looked at the door to the dining room. You were waiting for someone.

When I saw how you were waiting, how you wanted to stay and not to be left, then I believed you knew what you had done to me.

I stood up to leave. I stumbled as if I'd dropped something. You reached out to steady me but I pulled myself up. You placed your knitting on the chair and picked up your cane. You walked me to the door. We walked quietly so we wouldn't be heard. Now I could hear the clatter of plates in the kitchen. When you opened the front door, I heard a voice from the kitchen.

Is that you?

You didn't answer.

The voice sounded concerned the second time, afraid you were leaving. Is that you?

You tried to sound comforting. Yes, yes I'm just coming.

I walked out the door. As I was pulling it closed behind me, I felt your hand on mine.

Where are you going?

I'm going back to the city.

You started to say something else, but what you said was Goodbye.

When I closed the door behind me I felt you put your hands against it. Were you trying, with your hands, to touch the last thing of your house I'd left? We turned away from our separate sides of the door together. You walked with your cane to the dining room and I walked down the steps. I heard the scraping of chair legs on the floor, the clattering of silverware and plates, and then your common, ordinary voices.

I ran from the house through the unkept yard. The flashlight was shining beyond the open gate. She'd opened the gate to wait for me.

I'm sorry, I said, I didn't get anything.

Wasn't anything there?

Not what we needed.

She laughed with relief, Thank God. Her hand was on my arm.
Suddenly I wondered. Did you know whose house that was?
She nodded.
Why did you let me go in? I could have hacked —
You didn't, she said, You won't.

After that night we came to the ruined city.

The river that had borne the ruined city had run dry. We crossed the dry bed coughing dust. The city walls had fallen and the gate was gone. The lines on our skin got grey with ash. The sky was yellow. Nothing moved but us.

There's no one here.

There used to be.

Then I told her what I had denied about the city I'd not left entirely:

There were lots of us. It was a huge, thriving city. There was always traffic and there was this wonderful fountain everybody used to drive around in convertibles with the windows rolled down. It was always warm and sunny and we always sat at outdoor cafés. And everyone knew everyone and we never locked our doors. The windows were always open and even if you weren't out, you could hear your neighbors passing in the street and talking. Sometimes parties went on until dawn. Nobody had to wake up early and nobody had to work. We walked around in shorts and sandals and showed off our tans and our healthy skin and the firm tight muscles we got at the gym and our smooth, tough, flawless hands. At night we could end up anywhere and be, if not positively welcomed, at least politely tolerated. We couldn't imagine that the city hadn't always been the way we took for granted.

We couldn't imagine and then we couldn't believe, even when we saw what was happening to the two great beaches, the pretty canals, and all those cool cafés along the river. The first signs were innocuous – anglers grumbling they couldn't catch their limit, lifeguards competing for fewer jobs, and restless, sedentary children, the cafés on the waterfront complaining of the smell. But aside from a few old radicals who crawled out from under their rocks for the express purpose of babbling at us about these omens, no one gave these signs a second thought. And in fact, the warnings spouted by those archaic resisters from the underground actually contributed to our ignoring of the signs. We'd never liked listening to their puritan tales about the bad old days, the awful prophecies about the days to come. We didn't like their cheaply xeroxed flyers and their tacky tracts and the uncool designs of their posters. And we positively hated the holier-than-thou way they pointed at us, the arrogant show they made of their mutilations. They rambled on about a past that made no sense to us and accused us of not remembering our heritage. We dismissed their palsied waving of their scarred and gnarled hands. We turned up our dance tunes to drown out their ragings on about the sundering, the yellow sky, the bed of dust. But when they started moaning about babies stealing from mothers' mouths, and mothers selling babies for a cup, and sisters denying and lovers betraying and hacking and leaving and burying, that was the kind of talk we wouldn't tolerate. We gave them a choice: either Get out or Get out. And besides, we sneered, Wasn't it about time they heeded their own warnings? Shouldn't they make their great escape while they still could?

We let them pack while we scrambled around for the choicest seats from which to see them leave. They walked a desolate, slow migration, along the river's edge. They cried out to us to stop our fiddling and go with them. But we sat in the waterfront cafés, beneath the white-and-green Cinzano umbrellas that had always made us feel like movie stars, and sipped our drinks (which, to be honest, we had noticed were starting to get a bit skimpy). We fanned ourselves with copies of the tacky tracts they'd given us but that we had not read. They looked so dowdy clunking along in their sensible old maid shoes, their mannish overalls and ratty sweat-shirts. Their faces were black with sunscreen and their haircuts were unbelievably passé;

they never changed, they didn't keep up with the fashions. They stooped beneath their overloaded packs, their tin cups rattling like lepers' bells. We shouted Good Riddance and laughed Good Luck. And the one or two of us foolish enough to wave goodbye discovered, when she went to pick up her drink again, that one of her smiling neighbors had helped herself to it.

When the rationing began, each of us expected someone else to obey the measures. Everyone pretended to abide – we still respected appearances enough – but no one did. Everyone expected her more susceptible, gullible neighbors to make the sacrifice. Everyone assumed this odd aberration was a passing thing, would soon reverse, and we'd enjoy again the luxuries we thought were ours by right. We'd never had to do with less, we certainly didn't plan to start to now. So it was only after the fountains stopped, and after the grass turned brown, and only after the taps were dry, and when the bed was empty, that we saw our city might not be forever as it was.

Then suddenly we were desperate, and suddenly we discovered that our talk of generosity, of everybody's welcome right to everybody's good, was just the thoughtless, idle chatter of spoiled girls. We forgot the pretty promises that we'd all made when we'd all been so easily in love. We'd only pledged all our undying because we thought we'd never die. But then the soft, wet, open others' mouths which once had rendered us so blissfully, so breathlessly incapable of saying anything but Yes seemed to become voracious, deeper than a mine, and in ruthless competition for the poor rare drops we all so sorely needed.

We started lying about our needs, exaggerating our handicaps and pretending we had nothing we could spare. We hid what we had from our neighbors, then from our mothers and sisters, and finally from our precious, adorable babies. What we were one time smug enough to call our "universal, new and revolutionary love," we learned was only as sure – no – less – than our inconstant river.

Nobody wanted to see it go. We didn't want to admit what we were losing. Everyone stopped going out. Everybody stayed inside and huddled around her puny hoard. Though we'd never had a police force before, a guard was established to enforce the rationing. But these new civil servants only used their jobs to steal for themselves. Some of us tied ourselves to our canteens or tubs or bags so they couldn't carry off our tiny savings. But it wasn't long before even these most desperate measures proved useless against our former loved ones. They insisted we part with what we'd saved and they persuaded us. How they persuaded was: with hack saws and with cleavers and with knives. They brought their shovels and dug at us. Most of us were so afraid and tired and weak, and so horrified at what we had become, that we did not resist. The only ones who weren't completely shamed into inaction were the gangs.

The gangs of girls marched into where we lived like they were welcome. (And, to be fair, they had been once . . .) They knew from how they'd known us then where we kept what was dear to us. They knew where we hid our special secrets. But the sweet things we'd once said to them now mattered less than nothing. The terrible girls took anything that might contain a drop. We could hear them persuading, "Oh darling, please, just once, I'll never ask you again, I'll never – just a drop. Don't you remember the things you said, don't you remember what you did?" And then we'd hear this poor old frightened dame break down, in sentiment and terror and in the stupid, stupid hope that if she would cooperate, the terrible girls might spare her tits: They didn't.

At any time, at night or in the middle of the afternoon – they had no shame, they didn't even close the door – we could hear them going at it. We'd hear them beating and tearing at some poor wretch's scant reserve. And sometimes too, because we also had no shame, we'd peek through the blinds of our houses and watch them going at it. We'd watch them drag our neighbor into the street, or watch them have her in her private quarters.

We'd continue watching until she had been had to see what they cast off from her – a sleeve, a chunk, a thing sucked dry.

Sometimes some poor parched desperate maid who couldn't stand it any longer would leave her house to see if she could buy some. I'd hear her container bang against her leg as she hobbled down the street. But before she got too far from where she lived, they'd set upon her. I'd see what she carried snatched from her, and then her hands. I'd hear the slapping and tearing and teeth. The girls fought over what they stole – we'd never known we had such teeth and claws! – and they consumed, insatiably, all they could cram into their guts. They sold dregs for outrageous sums. A cup of it would buy a child. Then less—a spoonful, thimble, drop.

There was no defense against them, no defense against ourselves. We sat at home alone behind closed doors and hoped and prayed the terrible girls wouldn't find us.

I was among the last. Not because I was strong or brave, or because I had convictions. But because I was very good at waiting. And also because, unlike so many of my fellows, I didn't have that great pride of place that kept one on the right side of the river.

I knew I couldn't get far with what I had and I knew I couldn't go fast, my body was wrecked. But one night I snuck away from where we'd lived. I slid the silk sheets off my skin and tiptoed through the gallery and down the stairs. I weighed so little my feet were like air. I slipped out the front door and snuck along the street. I hid in openings and alleyways and I kept to the dark. I slunk past the place where the fountain had sprayed and crossed to the abandoned ghetto on the other side.

In a shabby hut at the end of a far-off alley, I hid. I closed the door behind me tight. Inside the hut was an obsolete old printer and stacks of yellowed paper. In a corner was a tattered mat. I lay on the mat to wait.

I woke when I heard them clattering down the alley. I got off the mat and went to the door. Through a crack in the door I saw them. The gang was small and the girls in it were scrawny, not as powerful as they had been once. Some of them swung empty sleeves and some of them were limping.

Though there wasn't much of me, the girls had come to this old part of town because they were desperate.

I sat as quiet as I could behind the door. I knew I couldn't hide forever but there was no place else to go. My only hope was that I might outlast them.

I sat as quiet as I could inside. I didn't move. But there was the sound of my breath; I held my breath. But there was the beating of my blood; and I could not hold that.

That's how they found me.

There was a knocking at the door.

I didn't answer but they knew I was there.

Hello, one of them said, It's me.

The others giggled.

I've brought you something.

She hit the door with something. They put their hands against the door and felt me inside. I couldn't hold them out. They busted in.

They pinned me down with their hands and knees. They trampled me.

When they'd torn me apart they let what was left of me fall. I curled up, pulling my knees to my chest as if I could contain what there still was of me.

They fought over it. They snatched it from each others' hands. Some of them put their mouths on it and others yanked it away. I heard it slip between their hands. They became so intoxicated with the fight that after a while they neglected what they were fighting over. When one of them dropped it, I pushed it beneath the mat. They were so busy making their ludicrous threats: Would you like to step outside to settle this? They didn't notice. I was relieved when they went outside.

I didn't yell at them. I didn't call them traitors or stupid bitches because I knew they hadn't enough to keep knocking each other around the way they were. I was happy to let them do what they did to each other. I was happy to hear the soggy sound of them beating and kicking and trampling the fucking shit out of one another.

It was a long time before I could sit up. I sat up carefully, trying to hold what remained of me together. I looked out the hole where the door had been. There were stains on the ground where they'd fallen. But the terrible girls were gone.

Inside the place I'd hid was wrecked. I crawled to the corner. I lifted the edge of the mat. Beneath it, like the wallflower ignored at the fancy ball – Oh what the terrible girls had left.

I swore, I vowed, and I have always kept each vow I've ever made, that if I ever laid eyes on one of the terrible girls again, I'd do the same true unforgivable thing to her. This was the greatest desire, the greatest desire that I have ever known. I longed to skewer those little rat's-assed bitches' asses up. I longed to string up the severed parts of them and watch them rot. But I knew if I achieved this true desire of my heart, I wouldn't be able to live with what I'd done.

So I had to get away. I had to get away from where I might be able to do what I wanted to them. I tried to pick up what they'd hacked from me but I was weak and it was very heavy. I couldn't carry it. And so I left it.

I tried to hide it, to protect it. I wrapped it around and tied it tight and put it where, when they came back, and I knew they would, they hadn't gone far, they hadn't gone more than a few hours walk from the city, I put it where I prayed they wouldn't find it. I dropped it down. I covered it. I left no sign. I left it in the dark. I left the city.

We came back to get what you left, she said.

There's nothing here. I didn't know if I lied.

There is. You left it here. You buried it. Tell me you buried it.

But I couldn't tell her what I did.

Take this off, she said.

I loosened the tie of the pack. She lifted it off my shoulders. I felt the sudden coolness of air on the sweat of my shirt. She took the pack off and set it on the ground.

We have to clear this junk away.

We stood in the ruins of where I had lived. Nothing was left whole. There were piles of brick and rubble. There were rags and charred black bits. I felt as weak as when I'd left.

She insisted, We have to clear it away.

We dragged the wreckage aside. When the ground was clear she listened. I heard nothing. She slowly walked to a certain place. She squatted down. Her hands began to make slow circles in the air above the ground. I stood behind her and watched her hands. She kept the circle of movement constant then lay her hands on the ground.

Here.

She started digging. I heard her fingers scrape the surface then the dry dirt crumble. The back of her neck was tight. Her arms were tense. She opened the earth and reached down in and lifted earth out. The dirt she pulled up was pale, then further down it got dark where it was moist. She tossed a bit of rope in the pile of dirt. Then her hands got something. She tried to pull it but it wouldn't move but she kept pulling. She kept her hands around the thing that would not move and made it move.

I flinched away. From the corner of my eye I saw her digging an opening like a trench around what she'd discovered. Then she was tugging.

Help me.

I didn't.

It's yours, she said.

She was kneeling on the ground. Her head was lowered. I didn't look at what she held but I saw her trembling arms. She was trying not to drop what she uncovered.

Why do you want it? I asked her.

Her back dropped. She struggled to hold it. It was hard for her to speak.

I wanted you to love me.

She was trying to lift it but she couldn't.

Help me.

Look at it, I said, though I didn't look. It's been down below so long. It's changed. It won't be what it was again.

I know, she said, Help me.

I thought she didn't understand me.

I can't love like that again, I said, I can't love you like that.

She held it still. I know that now, she said. But we came here to get it. It's yours. And I want how you can.

She tried to pull it up but she could not alone.

Help me.

I didn't know how but I wanted to do what she wanted. I kneeled beside her on the ground. I didn't look at it but I put my hand under hers and helped her move it. It was hard to lift. But our hands together removed it from its burial place.

We lay it on the ground.

I didn't look at it but I saw on the ground around it patches like leather that flaked off.

Take off your clothes.

I pulled them off. My back and stomach were wet with sweat.

Lie down.

I lay my clothes on the ground then I lay down. I felt chunks of earth crumble beneath me.

Close your eyes.

When I closed my eyes it was as dark as underneath the ground. I heard a familiar scraping sound, but it wasn't that, it was her scraping away what remained of the bag. I could hear her hands, I could almost see them pulling apart the last of the skin of the bag.

My skin was cold. The air was dry but I was sweating; her hands would slip.

I heard the moving of her hands, the mystery of her patient preparations. She said, Believe this telling of the tongue:

There is a sundering of blood
There is the carrying of loss.
There is the burial in earth.
There is the waiting in the dark.

There is the laying on of hands.
There is the opening of flesh.
There is the light within the body.
There is the resurrected heart.

And though my eyes were closed and though it was the starless night, I sensed a light was over me, right where she was, but in that light was a loss of light, a shadow, over me. Then I felt it lowering, then something cold against my skin. I felt it slipping on my skin and weighing down, then I felt an edge of something sharp, again, against where what had been hacked out of me was hacked.

There was something against my body, there was an opening, a blaze, there was the heart.

Ferlinghetti, L., ed. ENDS & BEGINNINGS (City Lights Review #6)
Ferlinghetti, L. PICTURES OF THE GONE WORLD
Finley, Karen. SHOCK TREATMENT
Ford, Charles Henri. OUT OF THE LABYRINTH: Selected Poems
Franzen, Cola, transl. POEMS OF ARAB ANDALUSIA
Frym, Gloria. DISTANCE NO OBJECT
García Lorca, Federico. BARBAROUS NIGHTS: Legends & Plays
García Lorca, Federico. ODE TO WALT WHITMAN & OTHER POEMS
García Lorca, Federico. POEM OF THE DEEP SONG
Garon, Paul. BLUES & THE POETIC SPIRIT
Gil de Biedma, Jaime. LONGING: SELECTED POEMS
Ginsberg, Allen. THE FALL OF AMERICA
Ginsberg, Allen. HOWL & OTHER POEMS
Ginsberg, Allen. KADDISH & OTHER POEMS
Ginsberg, Allen. MIND BREATHS
Ginsberg, Allen. PLANET NEWS
Ginsberg, Allen. PLUTONIAN ODE
Ginsberg, Allen. REALITY SANDWICHES
Glave, Thomas. WHOSE SONG? And Other Stories
Goethe, J. W. von. TALES FOR TRANSFORMATION
Gómez-Peña, Guillermo. THE NEW WORLD BORDER
Gómez-Peña, Guillermo, Enrique Chagoya, Felicia Rice. CODEX ESPANGLIENSIS
Goytisolo, Juan. LANDSCAPES OF WAR
Goytisolo. Juan. THE MARX FAMILY SAGA
Guillén, Jorge. HORSES IN THE AIR AND OTHER POEMS
Hagedorn, Jessica. DANGER & BEAUTY
Hammond, Paul. CONSTELLATIONS OF MIRÓ, BRETON
Hammond, Paul. THE SHADOW AND ITS SHADOW: Surrealist Writings on Cinema
Harryman, Carla. THERE NEVER WAS A ROSE WITHOUT A THORN
Herron, Don. THE DASHIELL HAMMETT TOUR: A Guidebook
Higman, Perry, tr. LOVE POEMS FROM SPAIN AND SPANISH AMERICA
Hinojosa, Francisco. HECTIC ETHICS
Jaffe, Harold. EROS: ANTI-EROS
Jenkins, Edith. AGAINST A FIELD SINISTER
Katzenberger, Elaine, ed. FIRST WORLD, HA HA HA!: The Zapatista Challenge
Keenan, Larry. POSTCARDS FROM THE UNDERGROUND: Portraits of the Beat Generation
Kerouac, Jack. BOOK OF DREAMS
Kerouac, Jack. POMES ALL SIZES
Kerouac, Jack. SCATTERED POEMS
Kerouac, Jack. SCRIPTURE OF THE GOLDEN ETERNITY
Kirkland, Will. GYPSY CANTE: Deep Song of the Caves
Lacarrière, Jacques. THE GNOSTICS
La Duke, Betty. COMPAÑERAS
La Loca. ADVENTURES ON THE ISLE OF ADOLESCENCE
Lamantia, Philip. BED OF SPHINXES: SELECTED POEMS
Lavín, Mónica, ed. POINTS OF DEPARTURE: New Stories from Mexico
Laure. THE COLLECTED WRITINGS
Le Brun, Annie. SADE: On the Brink of the Abyss
Lucarelli, Carlo. ALMOST BLUE
Mackey, Nathaniel. ATET A.D.
Mackey, Nathaniel. SCHOOL OF UDHRA
Mackey, Nathaniel. WHATSAID SERIF
Manchette, Jean-Patrick. THREE TO KILL
Maraini, Toni. SEALED IN STONE
Martín Gaite, Carmen. THE BACK ROOM
Masereel, Frans. PASSIONATE JOURNEY
Mayakovsky, Vladimir. LISTEN! EARLY POEMS
Mehmedinovic, Semezdin. SARAJEVO BLUES
Meltzer, David. SAN FRANCISCO BEAT: Talking with the Poets
Mension, Jean-Michel. THE TRIBE
Minghelli, Marina. MEDUSA: The Fourth Kingdom
Morgan, William. BEAT GENERATION IN NEW YORK

Mrabet, Mohammed. THE BOY WHO SET THE FIRE
Mrabet, Mohammed. THE LEMON
Mrabet, Mohammed. LOVE WITH A FEW HAIRS
Mrabet, Mohammed. M'HASHISH
Murguía, A. & B. Paschke, eds. VOLCAN: Poems from Central America
Nadir, Shams. THE ASTROLABE OF THE SEA
O'Hara, Frank. LUNCH POEMS
Pacheco, José Emilio. CITY OF MEMORY AND OTHER POEMS
Parenti, Michael. AGAINST EMPIRE
Parenti, Michael. AMERICA BESIEGED
Parenti, Michael. BLACKSHIRTS & REDS
Parenti, Michael. DIRTY TRUTHS
Parenti, Michael. HISTORY AS MYSTERY
Pasolini, Pier Paolo. ROMAN POEMS
Pessoa, Fernando. ALWAYS ASTONISHED
Pessoa, Fernando. POEMS OF FERNANDO PESSOA
Poe, Edgar Allan. THE UNKNOWN POE
Ponte, Antonio José. IN THE COLD OF THE MALECÓN
Porta, Antonio. KISSES FROM ANOTHER DREAM
Prévert, Jacques. PAROLES
Purdy, James. THE CANDLES OF YOUR EYES
Purdy, James. GARMENTS THE LIVING WEAR
Purdy, James. IN A SHALLOW GRAVE
Purdy, James. OUT WITH THE STARS
Rachlin, Nahid. THE HEART'S DESIRE
Rachlin, Nahid. MARRIED TO A STRANGER
Rachlin, Nahid. VEILS: SHORT STORIES
Reed, Jeremy. DELIRIUM: An Interpretation of Arthur Rimbaud
Reed, Jeremy. RED-HAIRED ANDROID
Rey Rosa, Rodrigo. THE BEGGAR'S KNIFE
Rey Rosa, Rodrigo. DUST ON HER TONGUE
Rigaud, Milo. SECRETS OF VOODOO
Rodríguez, Artemio and Herrera, Juan Felipe. LOTERIA CARDS AND FORTUNE POEMS
Ross, Dorien. RETURNING TO A
Ruy Sánchez, Alberto. MOGADOR
Saadawi, Nawal El. MEMOIRS OF A WOMAN DOCTOR
Sawyer-Lauçanno, Christopher. THE CONTINUAL PILGRIMAGE: American Writers in Paris
Sawyer-Lauçanno, Christopher, transl. THE DESTRUCTION OF THE JAGUAR
Scholder, Amy, ed. CRITICAL CONDITION: Women on the Edge of Violence
Schelling, Andrew, tr. CANE GROVES OF NARMADA RIVER: Erotic Poems from Old India
Serge, Victor. RESISTANCE
Shepard, Sam. MOTEL CHRONICLES
Shepard, Sam. FOOL FOR LOVE & THE SAD LAMENT OF PECOS BILL
Solnit, Rebecca. SECRET EXHIBITION: Six California Artists
Tabucchi, Antonio. DREAMS OF DREAMS & THE LAST THREE DAYS OF FERNANDO PESSOA
Takahashi, Mutsuo. SLEEPING SINNING FALLING
Turyn, Anne, ed. TOP TOP STORIES
Tutuola, Amos. SIMBI & THE SATYR OF THE DARK JUNGLE
Ulin, David. ANOTHER CITY: Writing from Los Angeles
Ullman, Ellen. CLOSE TO THE MACHINE: Technophilia and Its Discontents
Valaoritis, Nanos. MY AFTERLIFE GUARANTEED
VandenBroeck, André. BREAKING THROUGH
Vega, Janine Pommy. TRACKING THE SERPENT
Veltri, George. NICE BOY
Waldman, Anne. FAST SPEAKING WOMAN
Wilson, Colin. POETRY AND MYSTICISM
Wilson, John. INK ON PAPER: Poems on Chinese and Japanese Paintings
Wilson, Peter Lamborn. PLOUGHING THE CLOUDS
Wilson, Peter Lamborn. SACRED DRIFT
Wynne, John. THE OTHER WORLD
Zamora, Daisy. RIVERBED OF MEMORY